"THREE . . . TWO . . . ONE. ENGAGE WARP NOW, MR. SULU."

Sulu lightly tapped the switches as Mr. Spock spoke the word "engage," and the *Enterprise* surged forward, the stars blurring, the low rumbling of the massive engines rising through the walls and floor of the bridge.

A half second later, the *Sphinx* leapt on to the main viewing screen, and Sulu felt a burst of pride, the small ship less than twelve kilometers to port and only seven kilometers behind. He eased the *Enterprise* toward her, watching his console rather than the viewscreen—

—and felt his pride dissolve as he realized what was happening, even as Mr. Spock reported it to the captain. A glance at the screen confirmed it, the obviously impaired ship spewing a misty, ragged cloud of escaping gases, barely visible as it was torn away by warp—but it was just enough to disturb the *Sphinx*'s velocity constant.

And we can't hold a tractor beam in warp without a precise velocity match.

"In addition to their damaged core, it appears that their oxygen stores have been ruptured. The continued expulsion of gases and fuel is causing an erratic and unascertainable flight pattern," Mr. Spock said. "The possibility of achieving an exact parallel to its course is no longer a viable option."

STAR TREK®

SECTION 31™

CLOAK

S.D. PERRY

Based upon STAR TREK
created by Gene Roddenberry

POCKET BOOKS
New York London Toronto Sydney Singapore

An *Original* Publication of POCKET BOOKS

POCKET BOOKS, a division of Simon & Schuster, Inc.
1230 Avenue of the Americas, New York, NY 10020

ISBN: 0-671-77471-9

First Pocket Books printing July 2001

10 9 8 7 6 5 4 3 2 1

POCKET and colophon are registered trademarks of
Simon & Schuster, Inc.

Printed in the U.S.A.

For the writers of the original series, who made history

ACKNOWLEDGMENTS

A few of the people who helped to make this book possible are: Dr. Joelle Murray, my only science-savvy friend, whose facts I keep messing with; Mÿk Olsen, my husband, who keeps me sane, for the most part; Michael and Denise Okuda, for the brilliant encyclopedia and chronology, which kept me from drowning; and Marco Palmieri, my editor, who deserves most of the credit for this novel's outline, and a vacation.

Together let us beat this ample field,
Try what the open, what the covert yield.

—ALEXANDER POPE

CLOAK

Prologue

Jack Casden was having a nightmare, one he couldn't wake from because he wasn't asleep. Alone on the bridge, cut off from the rest of the ship, nothing responding to his commands—the only thing missing from this particular bad dream was some slithering and evil monster, although Casden was quite aware that monsters came in many forms, some of them as human as he was. To complete his nightmare, the incrementally rising, reedy whine of the warp engines humming through the walls and floor told him that it wouldn't be long now, not long at all. An hour, give or take. He'd be dead by then, anyway.

Casden took a deep breath, yet another in a series of deep breaths that wouldn't sustain him much longer, that barely sustained him now. No one was answering their communicators anymore, his last contact forty minutes before, with a dying ensign who was locked in her quarters. The very thought of it made him sick and weary, though he had no doubt he'd be sleeping soon enough, and for eternity; the only question was which would hold out longer, the air or the ship herself.

Was it worth it? Worth losing everything, just to die alone in the middle of nowhere?

There wasn't an answer; the question as futile as his situation. If he'd seen it coming, if he hadn't acted so rashly, if he'd given some thought to politics earlier in his career . . . worrying about what he might have done to make things different was useless in the here and now, it only worked to stoke the fires of his panic, and his self-control was all he had left. Everything else—his ship, his crew, his reputation—was gone, lost to his mistakes and those men and women who had exploited them.

Desperate, Casden held himself tighter against the growing cold, returning to theories and plans that he'd already rejected as impossible, sorting through them just to reject them again; short of giving up, it was all he could do. The ship's computer wouldn't answer, all bridge controls were locked out and unresponsive, and the subspace communications arrays had been damaged beyond repair. Even if he could find a way to record what was happening, to somehow explain himself, the ship was at warp five or six already and rising, he could tell by the sound; he figured she would blow up before she shook apart, and either way, there would be nothing left of her.

The bridge life-support had been cut last; his crew was surely dead. He didn't want to think about it, didn't want to live his last moments in total despair, but there was no help for the dense and dark responsibility that would serve as his shroud. Thirty-six people, men and women who had been his family for the last four years, trapped and asphyxiated. And all because of him, because of his stubborn inability to accept the truth. Because he hadn't opened his eyes until it was too late.

Behind him, the doors to the lift swished open, and there stood the unwelcome passenger, phaser in hand. A personal oxygen filter was fixed across his lower face, but Casden could see the glitter of false apology in his dark blue eyes.

From the station—

"I'm sorry about this," he said, and before Casden could think twice, he was rushing at the bastard, cold and dizzy and determined to take down the man responsible for the nightmare, his own life hardly worth saving in the face of what he'd helped create.

Chapter One

Captain's Log, Stardate 5462.1:
Having completed our survey to the edge of the Federation's recently incorporated Lantaru sector, we are now turning back toward more populated space. A Federation science summit is being held on Deep Space Station M-20 in two days; senior science officers and engineers from most of the ships in the quadrant are expected to attend, as well as several top Federation research scientists.

Dr. McCoy and the medical staff have begun their biannual physical workups for each crew member; I expect his initial report within the week.

On the bridge of the *Enterprise*, Captain James T. Kirk sat back in his chair, glad that he wouldn't have to endure yet another physical. It often seemed as if he had to go the rounds with McCoy's machinery every month or so, and as often as he ended up getting knocked around, being prodded and poked one more time wasn't high on his list of things to do. He'd been thoroughly checked out after the trouble with the interphase phenomenon and the Tholians only a few weeks ago, and Bones had declared him fit as a fiddle.

Well, except for being overworked, Kirk thought, gazing absently at the stars coursing by on the main viewscreen, passing at a leisurely warp four. Undoubtedly one of the constants in McCoy's reports—Bones loved to point out that the captain of the *Enterprise* needed to schedule himself a real vacation, or something dramatic and terrible might happen. Kirk liked to point out in turn that the ship's chief medical officer hadn't taken one in just as long, but Bones somehow managed to avoid hearing that part. The man was as stubborn as stubborn got.

Kirk smiled, just a little; one had to admire his tenacity, anyway. The science conference might allow both of them a break, at least for a couple of days; the main theme was to be the Federation's development of alternative power sources, much better suited to Spock or Scotty's area of interest than either of their own. Even at warp four they'd arrive a half day early, and technically, there would be nothing they *had* to do . . . however Bones felt about it, Kirk knew that a change of scenery would do him some good, not to mention a few reunions he was looking forward to—he wasn't sure about Commodore Mendez, but thought that Bob Wesley's ship was in the sector, and had heard that Gage Darres was assigned to M-20. It would be nice to see a few familiar faces—

"Captain, I'm picking up a signal from a Federation ship . . ."

Behind him, Lieutenant Uhura's voice was as cool and collected as always, but with a thread of tension that snapped Kirk out of his meandering reverie.

". . . it's the automated distress call of the *U.S.S. Sphinx,* condition red, disaster status," Uhura said, and Kirk was on his feet. At his station, Spock's hands were already moving, adjusting the ship's sensors to seek out the vessel.

The automated disaster signal only kicked in when there was no one to stop it from kicking in. Kirk quickly ran through the most likely possibilities as Uhura accessed stats, not liking any of them—*Plague. Hostile takeover. Antimatter breach. Another damned planet killer . . .*

"*U.S.S. Sphinx,* Centaurus-class starship, Captain Jack Casden commanding," Uhura said.

"How many aboard?" Kirk asked, unable to deny a small measure of relief. Centaurus vessels were primarily used for either scout or ambassadorial transport, occasionally as scientific surveyors, though not as processors; they were built for speed, and were among the smallest of the Federation's warp-capable ships. A Centaurus-class couldn't carry more than a hundred people.

"Crew list is thirty-seven, sir."

"Speed and bearing?" Kirk asked, stepping forward to look over Sulu's shoulder.

"It's traveling at . . . warp seven, from the Lantaru sector," Sulu said. "Headed 221 mark 35."

Damn. It was more or less aimed at a cluster of Federation civilian colonies in the Ramatis system, less than an hour away at that speed.

"Can you open a channel?" Kirk asked, turning to look at Uhura. She held her earpiece in place with one hand, deftly manipulating her station's receptors with the other.

"Negative, sir. Subspace arrays aren't receiving."

Bent over his station, Spock read off information from his console. "I'm picking up evidence of expelled warp plasma and debris trailing behind the ship." Spock straightened, turning to face him. "Captain, the *Sphinx* is in an increasing acceleration pattern. It is now traveling at warp eight, and will reach warp nine in three minutes, twenty-two seconds at its current rate of increase."

The Centaurus-class was made to be fast, but not that fast. She was damaged and dangerously out of control. Without knowing the status of the crew, they couldn't afford to risk damaging the ship any further—but they also couldn't let it get much closer to the heavily populated Ramatis system. She'd blow up before she reached it, but God only knew what was on board.

Kirk stepped to his chair, aware that he also couldn't afford to waste time considering the possibilities. It had been less than a minute since Uhura had reported the distress signal, but allowing another moment to pass without acting could mean death for Captain Casden and the people on his ship. If they were even alive; there was no way to scan for life signs without getting closer.

We have to get them out of warp, now. A dozen

half-formed thoughts darted through his deliberation before one evolved into an idea.

"Mr. Spock, assuming we can match their velocity, would it be possible to use the tractor beam to slow them down?" Kirk asked.

"It's possible, but it would have to be an exact match," Spock said. "Even a slight variance—"

"Mr. Chekov, lay in a parallel course," Kirk said, having heard all he needed to hear. It was a plan, simple but better than none at all, and if anyone could pull it off, his people could. "Mr. Spock, Mr. Sulu, I want you to coordinate with Mr. Scott, we're going to try and ease her out of subspace. Lieutenant, keep trying to raise them."

Kirk sat down as he spoke, barely hearing the acknowledgments around him, already hitting the chair's com with his right fist.

"Kirk to engineering. Scotty, we've got a situation."

"You want me to *what?*"

Standing next to the wall com with one hand on the switch, Scotty felt the too-familiar knot of anxiety and disbelief hit his gut and take hold, the captain's urgent explanation still ringing in his ears. Good Lord, what did he think the *Enterprise* was made out of, neutronium?

"You heard me. Spock's sending the numbers down now, and helm is standing by."

Scotty shook his head, the pulsing lights of the reaction chamber making his shadow spin at his feet. "Captain, I can get her up to speed, but there's no way to maintain it, not if you mean to use the tractor beam to—"

"Yes, I know, it's impossible," Kirk snapped. "And the longer you wait, the worse it's going to get. Do whatever it takes, Mr. Scott, but do it *now.*"

"Aye, sir, Scott out," Scotty said, turning to look at Grant and Washburn, seeing the same pained concern on their faces that he knew was on his own. It was just the three of them in main engineering, had been since lunch. Tam and Dixon were running diagnostics on the impulse drive and Celaux wasn't coming on for another half hour.

"You heard him, lads. Mr. Washburn, line up Mr. Spock's ratios and plug them in, then sit on the reaction chamber, watch for flux. And call in Celaux when you're done, put her on overrides and secondaries."

Scotty strode toward the warp-engine monitors deciding what they could spare, talking to Grant over his shoulder. "We're going to siphon from the phaser-bank reserves for the tractor beam. Get the transfer conduits primed and stand by, I'm going to see what I can do with the shields—"

"Sir, we're set to match," Washburn said. "They're at . . . eight-seven-four now."

"Distance from us?"

"61.280 billion kilometers and closing."

"Intersection?"

Washburn hesitated. "Uh . . . seventy-two million kilometers."

"Tell helm to set to mark at . . . eight-eight and a half," Scotty said, wincing inwardly, "and let Mr. Spock do the fine-tuning, we've got enough to do down here without hair-splitting." The bridge crew would have to be on their game, and to the millisecond; in a crunch, the *Enterprise* could reach nine-five without sustaining serious injury, but not for any sustained period of time, a certainly not with a beam on. Not unless Scotty wanted to cut life-support and AG, which he did not—and success or no, there wasn't going to be enough power for a second chance to catch the runaway. The captain could demand more power nine ways to Sunday, it wouldn't make a bit of difference.

Lieutenant Uhura's melodic voice floated hollowly through the chamber, a shipwide alert to secure positions. Scotty ignored it, figuring and entering a low-constant shield density into the boards, a part of him praying for the poor *Sphinx* and her crew, a part of him counting them lucky, indeed. If any ship in the galaxy could save her, surely it was the *Enterprise*.

"In twenty seconds, Mr. Sulu," Mr. Spock intoned.

Hikaru Sulu's fingers hovered over the warp-drive controls, watching science's readings for the runaway ship on his console, listening as Mr. Spock began to count down. Engineering said the *Enterprise* would be ready when the *Sphinx* reached high eight, 8.8550 to be exact. Rick Washburn and Mr. Spock had fed the numbers to Chekov, who had adjusted course before sending it on to helm—and although he knew he could trust the mathematics, it made Sulu nervous not to have time to go over their calculations. This was going to be one tricky bit of flying.

"Sixteen . . . fifteen . . ."

They would be jumping to match warp just before

the *Sphinx* passed them by, and although Sulu could easily slow the *Enterprise* down to fly alongside the runaway, having to speed up at all would throw the projections out of whack. Even without Mr. Scott's dire warnings, Sulu knew that the *Enterprise*'s entire energy output would be fully engaged—and since he would be piloting, he had to be as close to perfect as was possible.

"Eleven . . . ten . . ."

A lock of hair fell across his forehead, but he barely noticed, his full concentration on the task in front of him; he heard nothing but Mr. Spock's comfortingly bland voice, saw nothing but the dropping numbers on his screen, indicating the rapidly closing distance between the two ships. Mr. Scott would provide the power, Mr. Spock would handle the tractor beam, and the captain would give the commands—but it was up to him to fly straight and true, to bring them alongside the ailing ship so that they might save her from certain destruction.

"Three . . . two . . . one. Engage warp now, Mr. Sulu."

Sulu lightly tapped the switches as Mr. Spock spoke the word "engage," and the *Enterprise* surged forward, the stars blurring, the low rumbling of the massive engines rising through the walls and floor of the bridge.

A half second later, the *Sphinx* leapt on to the main viewing screen, and Sulu felt a burst of pride, the small ship less than twelve kilometers to port and only seven kilometers behind. He eased the *Enterprise* toward her, watching his console rather than the viewscreen—

—and felt his pride dissolve as he realized what was happening, even as Mr. Spock reported it to the captain. A glance at the screen confirmed it, the obviously impaired ship spewing a misty, ragged cloud of escaping gases, barely visible as it was torn away by warp—but it was just enough to disturb the *Sphinx*'s velocity constant. Sulu held his course and waited for instruction, wondering if Mr. Scott would be able to compensate, knowing already that it was practically impossible.

And we can't hold a tractor beam in warp without a precise velocity match. At best, the effort would be useless . . . and at worst, the beam could act like a battering ram, violently pushing the *Sphinx* away and causing more damage.

"In addition to their damaged core, it appears that their oxygen stores have been ruptured. The continued expulsion of gases and fuel is causing an erratic and unascertainable flight pattern," Mr. Spock said. "The possibility of achieving an exact parallel to its course is no longer a viable option."

Chapter Two

The captain stared at the viewscreen for a beat, frowning, then half-turned in his chair to look at Spock.

"Life signs?" he asked.

Spock glanced at his console once more, but there had been no change in the few seconds since he'd last checked.

"Readings are uncertain. I'm detecting several heat signatures, but they may be caused by mechanical overload. Life-support appears to be inactive."

"We have to stop that ship, Mr. Spock. What *can* we do?"

The captain's frustration was clear in his voice, but Spock had no immediate answer, not unless he interpreted the question literally—which was not, of course, what Captain Kirk wanted.

The *Sphinx* couldn't be boarded at warp, and the

next several most conspicuous choices involved jeopardizing either their crew or the *Enterprise*'s. While the available data suggested there was no life on board, there was doubt—and the possibility that even one crew member was still alive excluded a simple solution. Spock knew that the captain would reject endangering life if at all possible, an admirable if sometimes illogical predilection of his.

"Stabilizing the *Sphinx*'s flight pattern and proceeding with the original plan creates the least risk," Spock said, still considering alternatives as he spoke. "However, their systems aren't functioning to a degree that would allow for a remote computer interface or override."

The captain turned back to the screen, absently rubbing his jaw, an expression of intense thought narrowing his eyes. The faltering ship continued to vent a primarily oxygen-hydrogen crystalline fog from its aft compartments, a barely detectable emerging haze. Only a few seconds passed before he spoke, in the soft tone that generally defined his process of thinking aloud. The increasingly erratic sound of the laboring warp drive nearly drowned out his observation.

"Plasma bleeding out, and if the oxygen stores have ruptured, the leaks must be coming from cargo and lower engineering areas only. . . . If we could widen the breach without compromising any other compartments . . ."

Spock nodded, following the thought to its inevitable conclusion. "The expulsion would hasten and then cease, stabilizing their flight pattern."

"Scott to bridge." The engineer sounded hurried and tense.

The captain triggered the com. "Kirk here. Go ahead, Scotty."

"We've just passed warp nine, sir, and she's starting to strain. I can only give you another two, three minutes at most before we risk an overload."

"Which is it, two or three?"

A hesitation, then Mr. Scott's anxious reply. "I can promise you two. Much more than that is wishful thinking, sir."

Spock's own estimates were higher by just under a minute but he inwardly deferred to the engineer's appraisal, figuring it into matters. Though Mr. Scott's consistently emotional reaction to crisis was impractical, his competence was indisputable.

"What about the tractor beam?" the captain asked, frowning.

"We're running it off the phaser reserves."

The captain stood up, his stance and tone the epitome of command, his decision made.

"We have only one option, and not much time," he said firmly, raising his voice to be heard clearly over the engines. "Chekov, target a photon torpedo on that breach, lowest possible yield. Your aim is going to have to be absolutely precise, so don't lock until you're sure. I want to open that hole wider, not blow up the ship. Can you do it?"

Mr. Chekov straightened his shoulders, lifting his chin and lowering it in a brisk nod. His response suggested absolute confidence in his own abilities. "It's no problem, sir."

"Sulu, the instant the *Sphinx* is stable enough to

match, do it, don't wait for my command. Spock, same goes for you—I want that tractor beam locked on as soon as it's possible. Scotty, start decelerating the second we get a grip, slow and steady. We need absolute precision on this, gentlemen, so watch for your cues."

Spock acknowledged the orders along with the others, fascinated as always with the incredible self-assurance that the captain so easily projected . . . as well as his unwavering faith in the abilities of the people he commanded. By simply expecting their best, he somehow always managed to get it—as though the expectation itself inspired consistently peak performance.

In the years they'd served together, Spock had come to know that the captain was the inspiration, his crew proud to be under his command and motivated to meet his standards. In that, emotion played no small part . . . a small but compelling fact that Spock had pondered on more than one occasion, considering the things he had done or been willing to do for Jim Kirk.

"Torpedo locked on target," the navigator said, sounding no less sure of himself than when he'd accepted the challenge.

The captain stared hard at the screen, then nodded once.

"Fire," he said, and a burst of light flashed from the *Enterprise*, setting his plan into motion.

After establishing a repeating broadband explanation and instruction loop to the *Sphinx*, for what it was worth, Lieutenant Uhura cleared channels from all decks for activity reports and turned in her seat to look at the viewscreen. Until her next update to Starfleet, there was nothing to do but watch.

And pray, she amended silently, sending out a good thought for the troubled ship just as the captain gave the word and Mr. Chekov fired.

A bolt of brilliance and then the *Sphinx* was lurching wildly, a tiny boat on storming seas. It veered sharply from its course, perhaps pushed by the billow of freezing moisture and gas that erupted from its stern and instantly disappeared in the passing dark.

"Got it!" Chekov exclaimed, and though she couldn't see his face, she could hear boyish triumph in his voice, even over the intense rumbling and whining of the *Enterprise*'s engines.

"Stay with her, Mr. Sulu," Captain Kirk said, not taking his gaze from the screen. "Spock?"

"Mr. Chekov is correct," the Vulcan responded, the cool light from his console bathing his face in flickering green, his raised voice just as cool. "No suggestion of internal breach . . . and the sensors report a drastic decline in the ship's oxygen purge. The *Sphinx*'s flight should stabilize within—sixty seconds."

As if on cue, Mr. Scott's thick brogue spilled onto the bridge and into her ear simultaneously, stilling a short-lived flutter of hope. Uhura reflexively tuned out everything but what she heard from her own station, concentrating, holding the earpiece firmly in place in spite of the engineer's near shout.

"Captain, I can give you another minute, no more! I'm already pushing as hard as I can, there's nothing else I can do!"

The engineer's warnings over sustained high warp were no less terrifying for their familiarity. Uhura felt an icy hand clutch at her heart and drum its fingers there, the mental image of the *Enterprise*'s death clear in her mind, an image she'd once dreamed and had never forgotten—the starship rocketing through the freezing dark like a sculpture of ice, pieces of her shedding away as though she were melting, the final silent explosion and the scattering glitter of four hundred lives. So many people turned into so much dust as simply as that, tiny motes propelled forever through a black vacuum, far, far from home—

The captain spoke quickly. "Try crossing your fingers, Mr. Scott."

Even tense and frustrated, Captain Kirk had a gift for stilling her fears. Uhura took a deep breath and mentally crossed her own fingers.

The excruciating seconds ticked away, the sound of the *Enterprise*'s suffering engines becoming choppy, Sulu's back and shoulders stiff as he waited to do his part. Everyone else watched the screen anxiously except for Mr. Spock, still bent over his reader, one hand on the tractor-beam controls.

"Flight pattern is stabilizing," Mr. Spock said, and the laboring engines somehow managed to respond to Sulu's light touch, the painful, strained sound rising another impossible notch as the *Enterprise* slid forward, smoothly closing the gap.

The rest happened fast. Even as they appeared to match course next to the smaller ship, Mr. Scott shouted in Uhura's ear and across the bridge. "Captain, I'll have to shut it all down now or—"

"Just a few more seconds, Scotty," the captain interrupted, firmly but somehow absently, his entire focus on the *Sphinx*.

"Matched and locked," Sulu said.

Staring into his station's raised screen, Mr. Spock's right hand quickly tapped across several switches. "Tractor beam locked on, Captain."

Within a few seconds, the rumbling roar of their engines began to subside, easing back to warp eight, and Uhura remembered to breathe again. The small ship stayed with them as Mr. Scott slowly and steadily powered down the warp engines.

Captain Kirk turned, smiling, taking his seat as if the brief but dramatic encounter were a matter of routine. "Excellent work, gentlemen. Lieutenant, pass the word along to the crew, if you would . . ."

The captain kept talking, giving orders to helm and engineering, but Uhura was already on open com and barely heard him, concentrating on her work. She quickly relayed the information shipwide, speaking and listening at once as reports from every deck and department flooded in. Except for a few overheated circuit boards and drive coils in engineering, the *Enterprise* was undamaged.

Uhura stated as much to the captain and started logging the reports, relieved and grateful that the *Sphinx* had been saved. As always when danger presented itself and then left them, defeated, she was glad to be part of such a talented and resourceful crew—a feeling more than a thought, a kind of security that she only rarely acknowledged. Entering data into the computer was a simple task but one that required her full attention, so she wasn't thinking about herself or anything else as she worked—and she didn't pick up on what Mr. Spock was saying until Captain Kirk repeated it, his tone of dismay jolting her from her trance of efficiency.

"None? Spock, are you sure?"

"Quite," Mr. Spock replied, and though he displayed no emotion, the lines of his carefully stoic face seemed deeper somehow. "There are no survivors aboard the *Sphinx;* Captain Casden and his crew are dead."

Leonard McCoy reached the transporter room just in time to hear the tail end of the initial atmospheric report from one of Scotty's boys, his suit helmet in one hand. Ensign Burton or Burdock, McCoy couldn't remember, the kid was relatively new to the *Enterprise.* Spock was reading from the young man's tricorder while Jim listened intently, the trio standing near the transporter controls. The other engineering tech, Rick Washburn, was shedding his environmental suit in the far corner. Two security guards waited on the transporter platform.

". . . see anyone, but we didn't leave engineering, either," the young man was saying.

"We couldn't get out, the door was jammed from the outside," Washburn added. "It was definitely life-support failure, but it could've been fixed if someone had been able to get to it in time. It only took us twenty minutes."

"No sign of airborne toxins or disease," Spock said, snapping the tricorder off and slinging it over his shoulder as McCoy approached. The captain thanked and dismissed the two young men, nodding an unsmiling acknowledgment at McCoy.

And no wonder. A seemingly senseless tragedy, no rhyme or reason to it, and a mystery to boot. He knew Jim well enough to know he wouldn't rest until he got to the bottom of it . . . although he wasn't sure why the captain wanted him on the team. Or security guards, for that matter.

"Doctor," Spock said.

"I thought you said everyone on the *Sphinx* was dead," McCoy said mildly, addressing the captain but nodding politely at Spock in turn. It obviously wasn't a good day for sparring with the Vulcan, even if he wanted to.

Jim nodded once, his mouth set in a tight line. "They are, and it looks like life-support failure . . . but I want to know that for a fact."

McCoy tilted his head toward the security guards. "Are we expecting trouble?"

"No, but since we don't know how their computer is operating, we may need to search the ship room by room," he answered, stepping toward the transporters. "We need the extra eyes."

Spock and McCoy followed, taking places on either side of the captain, the doctor feeling the all-too-familiar unease as he stepped onto the platform. He suppressed his natural impulse to grumble about the transporter; if Spock overheard him, he'd have to sit through another damned lecture on science and safety statistics, a prospect even less appealing than being scrambled and reassembled by a computer.

"Energize," Jim said, nodding at the operator.

A shimmering haze, the thrumming of the transporter in operation, and they were standing on the bridge of the Centaurus-class starship, the rectangular room about half the size of the *Enterprise*'s bridge. Only the emergency lights appeared to be operating, the station consoles all lifeless, dark and silent—and it was cold, damn near freezing. Life-support was back on, maybe, but the new atmosphere obviously hadn't had time to warm up yet. McCoy scowled, his arms instantly pebbling—

—and forgot the cold as he saw the bodies. Two men in a sprawled heap not far from the bridge doors, half hidden by a standing console. One was in a command uniform, the other wearing an engineering jumpsuit.

"Bones," Jim said, but McCoy was already moving toward them, his medical tricorder and scanner in hand.

The doctor crouched next to the bodies, running the scanner over each, making his own observations as the tricorder processed the information. The man in uniform was a captain, presumably *the* captain, one Jack Casden. Casden held a broken oxygen mask in one hand, and had been hit in the chest by phaser fire at near point-blank range; the shot would have killed him instantly. The other man still clutched the offending weapon; he was cyanotic, and had died recently. From the cell deterioration, no more than two hours had passed since his death, presumably by asphyxiation.

McCoy bent closer to the engineer, studying his face. There was a slender thread of abraded skin that ran horizontally across the bridge of his nose . . . which would undoubtedly line up with the upper lip of the oxygen mask that the captain held in one frozen hand.

The engineer shot Casden, Casden broke the engineer's mask . . . but why? And who started it?

McCoy sat back on his heels, frowning, just as Spock piped up from one of the consoles that lined the far wall, his statement only adding to the mystery they'd beamed into.

"Captain, the ship's computer banks have been erased. Every recorded file has been deleted, from personnel records to maintenance reports."

"Mechanical failure?" Jim asked, looking as perplexed as McCoy felt.

"Negative," Spock said calmly. "From the chronological pattern of expungement, it could only be an act of sabotage."

McCoy looked back at the dead captain and his killer, the chill of his flesh nothing compared with the chill of apprehension that ran up his spine.

"What the hell happened here?" Jim asked softly, but no one answered, the *Sphinx* as enigmatically silent as its namesake.

Chapter Three

Ensigns Burdock and Washburn hadn't seen anyone in the *Sphinx*'s main engineering room because they hadn't looked in the supply closet. When Kirk finally managed to unjam the door—as deliberately jammed as the entrance to engineering had been—he found two men and a woman inside, engineers, huddled together and as cold as ice. They had suffocated, their lips and fingernails the same ghastly shade of blue as those of everyone else on board.

Except for Casden.

Killed by one of his own, and perhaps with reason. Kirk didn't want to consider it, but he couldn't help wondering if Bones was right. The doctor had put forth a disturbing theory before they'd split up to search the ship, suggesting that Casden had shut off life-support and then been tracked down and shot by a survivor, the engineer. It would certainly explain a few things, a mad captain destroying himself and taking his ship and crew with him—madness needed no motive—but it also raised even more questions, the logistics alone giving pause . . . and although he had nothing to back him up, no clear evidence, Kirk's instincts were telling him there was much more to the story behind the catastrophe, behind the terrible silence that had greeted their arrival.

He turned away from the pathetic trio in the supply closet, saddened and frustrated at the terrible waste, his heart pounding with it. The cold and poorly lit room was completely devoid of life, except for the mute blinking of the life-support controls across from him, a small handful of lights in a wall of equipment that should have been glittering with power. Knowing that the entire tragedy could have been avoided with just twenty minutes of work by a trained engineer, three of them trapped less than four meters away—it was intolerable.

An entire crew, dead, no accident and no explanation. Kirk walked slowly toward the live panel, thinking about the erased computer banks, wondering what they could have learned from the lost files. Spock had made it clear that it hadn't been a straight-across wipe, that some thought had gone into it . . .

. . . *and it doesn't fit. The kind of psychotic personality it would take, to commit mass murder and destroy your own ship—would that kind of man take the time and effort to selectively delete files? And if you meant to blow up your own ship, why bother deleting them at all?*

He stopped in front of the panel, staring down at it without really seeing, suddenly thinking about the routine physicals that McCoy was going to be conducting over the next few days. Thinking about the standard dermal-optic test required for all personnel, a test that would provide ample warning of an impending psychosis. People didn't just snap and turn violent, not without some lead-up, not unless it *was* some kind of an affliction or disease . . . but the tricorder readings showed nothing unusual. With the medical files erased, there was no way to tell when the *Sphinx* crew had last undergone any kind of psychiatric evaluation, but certainly not more than six months, and most starship captains had them quarterly—

His communicator signaled. Kirk flipped it open, its gentle cricket sound overly loud in the silent room.

"Kirk here."

"Spock here, Captain. The doctor and security personnel have returned to the bridge, reporting thirty-two deaths in addition to the two men here."

"Add three more to the count, Mr. Spock," Kirk said heavily, gazing at the repaired life-support system as he spoke. "I'm on my way now . . ."

He trailed off, peering closer at the console. The controls that regulated atmosphere and temperature, basic life-support, seemed barely damaged . . . though the panels next to it had been smashed to pieces, what could only be the reaction-chamber overrides—

—as though life-support wasn't the target at all.

"Spock . . . have Mr. Scott bring a team over to assess the physical damage to the ship," Kirk said slowly, not sure what he was looking for, not yet. "I want everything checked, bow to stern—and have him run tests for unusual energy fields or readings, anything out of the ordinary. Kirk out."

He took a final, lingering look at the three people curled together in death, hoping that there had been some comfort for them in not dying alone—and as he turned to leave engineering, he realized that he was angry, furious, in fact. Someone, some black and twisted mind, had plotted and carried out this senseless nightmare, making these people die cold and in the dark.

Kirk wouldn't—couldn't—let it go unpunished. If it was within his power, he would find out who was responsible and see that they were brought to justice, whatever it took. If it was Casden, he got off easy.

Although he was certain of his findings to a negligible percentage, Spock went through the entire process a second time—accessing the personnel files for each crew member of the *Sphinx* and cross-referencing them with Dr. McCoy's DNA samples, collected in their search of the small ship.

The science officer sat alone in a seldom-used conference room on deck nine, methodically reviewing each match with the computer. His presence was not required on the bridge, and though his quarters were certainly more comfortable than the room he'd chosen, he often preferred to work in such settings—the bland environment provided no distraction, and while his concentration skills weren't lacking, he'd found that the complete absence of aesthetic quality frequently enhanced his ability to focus.

When Spock had concluded his task a second

time, the results undeviating, he left the conference room and started for the bridge to tell the captain. The information was important, perhaps crucial to the *Sphinx* investigation, and Spock also wanted leave to return to the ship; his discovery required another search.

He reached a turbolift and stepped on, requesting the bridge. Alone on the lift, his thoughts centered around several interesting possibilities he hadn't yet explored, as to the creation of the *Sphinx's* current circumstances. Unfortunately, he didn't have enough information to fully consider any one of them—and though a number of his theories were highly improbable, he couldn't decisively exclude any, either. Engineer Scott's report would undoubtedly change things.

The atmosphere on the bridge was subdued, certainly an emotional reaction to the loss of life. The captain sat stiffly in his chair, resting his chin in one hand as he stared at the main screen, at the powerless *Sphinx* floating nearby. When he noted Spock's appearance, he quickly stood.

"What have you got?"

"Assuming that Dr. McCoy's DNA samples from the *Sphinx's* crew were properly gathered—and I have no reason to believe they were not—the human male responsible for shooting Captain Casden was not a member of his crew, nor is he registered in any Starfleet database. At present, I am unable to identify him."

The captain frowned, considering the information. The *Enterprise's* medical library was extensive, maintaining a current DNA database for all Starfleet personnel, as well as a vast, ever-growing medical catalogue of Federation members. Anonymity was not rare, but an unidentified human on a starship was. Starfleet required that all non-Federation passengers on warp-capable vessels be reported.

"What about the rest of the crew?" the captain asked.

"All accounted for. Thirty-seven, including Jack Casden."

"Last assignment?"

"That is unclear," Spock said. "It appears they were due for ship leave, following a routine equipment drop for the Vega colony. The closest Federation stations to their last reported location were Starbase 19 and Deep Space Station R-5, but they are not listed as having docked at either."

The captain's frown deepened. "That's a long way from here. Have you estimated their point of origin?"

"Uninhabited space, deep in the Lantaru sector," Spock replied. "No colonies or planets capable of sustaining life within two light-years."

The captain shook his head, an expression of frustration on his face. "It sounds like our best bet is to figure out who their mystery guest was, wouldn't you agree?"

A logical conclusion. "Indeed. I would like permission to return to the *Sphinx,* to see if I can ascertain the unidentified man's quarters. Perhaps a search of his belongings—"

"Permission granted. And see if you can help Mr. Scott hurry things along while you're over there, I expected his report twenty minutes ago."

Spock nodded assent and turned to leave, just as the captain's intercom signaled. It was Mr. Scott, calling from the *Enterprise* transporter room.

"Report," the captain said, and Spock stopped to listen, curious. The unusual developments thus far had been most interesting, and it was reasonable to anticipate further irregularities in their investigation. What the engineer had to say, however, was entirely unexpected.

"Captain, the damage inside her wasn't anything out of the ordinary, mostly what we already thought," Mr. Scott said, his tone one of barely restrained excitement. "Subspace communications were knocked out, and it does look like warp and navigation controls were the main targets . . . but you'll never guess what we found on her hull—"

"Scotty . . ." The warning was inherent in the captain's irritable interruption.

"The *Sphinx* has recently been exposed to a graviton field," the engineer said, sounding as though he believed his statement was of unusual importance.

The captain cocked an eyebrow at Spock, who took the initiative. "Mr. Scott, naturally occurring graviton fields are extremely common, and quite harmless. That a ship traveling over such a distance might be exposed to—"

"Aye, aye, I'm not daft, Mr. Spock," the engineer said, with great exasperation. Spock was about to state that he wasn't trying to insinuate otherwise when Mr. Scott expanded on his original statement.

"It's the *type* of graviton field. A while ago, when we met up with the Romulans and, ah, *borrowed* their cloaking device—for a short time after we used it, the hull of the *Enterprise* had the same kind of readings. Exactly the same, and the readings are like no other, there's no mistaking them for something else. There's not any evidence of such a device being used by the *Sphinx,* but I'd bet my own mother's good name that she's been inside a Romulan cloaking field, and recently."

In spite of the confusing grammar—obviously, "she" was the *Sphinx,* rather than Mr. Scott's mother—the revelation was significant, to say the least. Whatever the circumstances in which the *Sphinx* was exposed to a cloak, the implications, for the Federation as well as for Captain Casden, were potentially devastating.

"Fascinating," Spock said, and from the look on the captain's face, he wasn't the only one who thought so.

Ever since the *Enterprise*'s trip to the Gamma Hydra IV colony, and his fortunate resistance to the accelerated aging disease, Pavel Chekov was basically unnerved by even routine visits to sickbay. Not that he would ever admit to it, of course, he had his pride to think of, but those long, torturous hours of playing specimen had been hard to shake. And although he liked Dr. McCoy well enough, the words "just one more sample, Chekov" still haunted him occasionally, usually in anxiety dreams that also included him forgetting where his final Academy exam was being held.

Well, at least I'm near the beginning. Less time to dread it, he thought, standing outside sickbay. Right after Chase, just before Chesterton; five to ten minutes of physical and psychological testing and he could go back to the bridge, finished for another six months. It was where he wanted to be, anyway, considering what Mr. Spock and the captain had been talking about when he'd left—

The doors to sickbay swished open and Steve Chase stepped out, almost walking right into him. Embarrassed, Chekov excused himself, squared his shoulders, and stepped inside before the doors closed.

Christine Chapel was standing near the exam table, writing something on a clipboard. She looked up and smiled at him, her eternally sincere kindness easing some of his apprehension. A very nice lady, Nurse Chapel.

"Right on time, Mr. Chekov," she said, and nodded toward the table. "Dr. McCoy is just making some notes, but we can go ahead and get your blood pressure and weight . . ."

Chekov held his head high as he approached the table, reminding himself that Russia was the birthplace of modern medicine, that his own ancestors had no doubt helped create the diagnostic pad he was about to lie down upon. He boosted himself onto the table, the medical indicators coming to life as his head hit the pillow, loudly beeping and bleating his vitals into the room. Even he could tell that his heart rate was high, the skittering *thum-thump* audibly betraying his nervousness.

"Relax, Pavel," Nurse Chapel said, her voice soothing. "Breathe evenly, and try to think of someplace nice." She pressed a button on her clipboard and started recording.

"I *am* relaxed," he grumbled, but took a few deep breaths anyway, forcing his muscles to unclench.

"Let me guess—the Russians invented meditation," Dr. McCoy said amusedly, entering from the next room.

Chekov shook his head. "No, but they perfected it, on Earth in the early twenty-first century. We are a very spiritual people, you know."

"I don't doubt it," McCoy said, picking up a tricorder and scanner from the nearby countertop and stepping closer to the table.

Chekov cast about for something to say, to keep his mind from dredging up anxious memories. "So . . . does the medical staff also have their physical tests alphabetically?"

Nurse Chapel answered, smiling. "Actually, no. We just fit them in somewhere along the way. I had mine this morning, when Dr. M'Benga was filling in. Right between A and B."

"That's right—you were on the *Sphinx,* weren't you?" Chekov asked McCoy, curiosity outpacing his nervousness. "Did you hear about the stranger, the one who killed the captain?"

McCoy nodded, though his nurse seemed confused. "Captain Kirk just called," McCoy explained, frowning slightly at Chekov. "It seems there was no DNA match for one of the men on board . . . though I'm sure gossiping about it isn't going to help matters along."

"Yes, sir," Chekov said, though he wasn't quite ready to give up. "I *am* going to help, though, just as soon as I leave here. I'll figure out who he is, no problem."

"Sit up and take off your shirt," McCoy said, holding up his tricorder. Chekov was pulling his shirt over his head when the doctor caved. "And just how do you propose to do that, when he's not in the database?"

Chekov smiled proudly. "I have connections . . . and I'm also very good at tracking people down, through assignment files and reports. Everyone leaves a trail somewhere. It can be time-consuming, tracing someone like that, it takes patience and perseverance . . . but some of history's greatest detectives were Russian, you know, and—"

"And I'm sorry I asked," McCoy said, scowling. "Hop off, and let's get you on the treadmill before you blow yourself out."

Nurse Chapel made a coughing sound and turned away, but Chekov wasn't offended, smiling at the doctor as they moved toward the endurance test, a prone treadmill exercise. Really, having something to talk about allayed much of his fear, even if it did spark a reaction in Dr. McCoy. Jealousy came in many forms, and Chekov had learned long ago to accept and transcend it; not everyone could take pride in their heritage, but after all, they couldn't help their own ancestry.

Chapter Four

When Jim called the briefing, Dr. McCoy had just finished administering his own physical, excusing Nurse Chapel early to dinner in order to maintain some privacy. Doctors were the worst patients, himself included, so he quickly ran his tests before Nurse West came on, knowing that she'd try to convince him to let M'Benga examine him; he didn't want to spend a single minute getting riled up because M'Benga—an excellent doctor, to be sure—ran the tests differently than he would have, or treated him like a patient. If he wanted to be patronized, he'd spend more time with Spock.

McCoy included his data along with the C and D patients', racking the samples and plugging his tricorder into the lab computer for analysis only seconds before Jim called.

"Kirk to sickbay."

McCoy stepped to the com. "Yes, Jim."

"Bones, senior staff meeting, main briefing room. We need to talk about the *Sphinx,* and I want your opinion on something Spock found."

"What's that?"

A pause. "I'm not sure yet," Jim said.

Another mystery? The deaths, the stranger, the cloak reading . . . they had enough to deal with already.

"I'll be right there," McCoy said, glancing over at the processing computer. His patience was limited when it came to his own health, but it would take at least an hour for the samples to be tested for all the standards, longer if the computer picked up something exotic. He'd go to the meeting, have dinner, and check the reports before bed, the prospect of an early evening feeling more like a necessity than a choice.

Admit it, Doctor, you're not happy with your endurance results. You're getting older, that's all, no shame in that.

McCoy ignored the smarmy inner voice as he left sickbay and headed for the briefing, but he couldn't entirely ignore the rather disheartening thoughts it had raised. His last full physical, only six months ago, he'd had the stamina and lung capacity of a man in his early thirties, not too bad for a forty-plus geezer such as himself . . . but the three minutes of pedal-pushing he'd just suffered had felt like running up the side of a mountain with weights on.

And now I'm tired and my feet hurt, he thought, stepping onto the turbolift, *and if this is what I have to look forward to for the next hundred years or so . . .*

. . . you could *start watching what you eat and getting a little more exercise, you really should once you hit forty,* the smarmy voice interjected, but he'd already heard enough from *that* particular collection of brain cells.

Hell with it, he thought as the turbolift stopped on deck three, the doors opening, he'd retire soon enough and take up napping full-time, maybe invest in one of those personal all-terrain transports that the very old hopped around in back on Earth. He'd make house calls in style.

As he walked down the deck's main corridor to the briefing room, nodding at a few passing crew members, he realized that his feet actually *did* hurt. They felt swollen, edemic; maybe all he really needed was a new pair of boots and a vacation. Jim was always pointing out how much he needed a decent holiday, which was true, but also a fine example of the pot calling the kettle black. The captain turned a deaf ear to his chief medical officer's advice about taking a break, talk about *stubborn.*

McCoy walked into the briefing room and took his seat, nodding pleasantly at Sulu and Uhura, who were chatting about one of the helmsman's botany experiments. Mr. Scott sat across the table from him, looking a little worn out. After the afternoon he'd had, McCoy wasn't surprised; the engineer worked miracles with warp drive, lucky for all of them, but excluding the captain's, his job was probably the most consistently stressful on board.

Jim and Spock showed up a moment later, Spock carrying a very small, very damaged-looking data chip that he set on the table before sitting down. The captain remained standing. McCoy recognized the look of absolute determination on Jim's face, his eyes sparking with an almost rebellious intensity, and wondered if he'd talked to Starfleet yet.

The captain nodded at Spock, who picked up the chip again, passing it to Mr. Scott.

"Several hours ago, I discovered this information chip on board the *Sphinx*," Spock said, "which I believe belonged to the unidentified killer of Captain Casden. The chip was in a storage locker in an unused compartment, along with packs of field rations, bottled water, and several tools—the hiding place of a stowaway saboteur, perhaps. Trace DNA from the unknown man was found on the locker, and on the chip itself. As you can see, the chip has been badly damaged, melted beyond the point of functionality."

Scott passed the chip to McCoy, who knew the punch line already. "And yet somehow, you managed to make it function, didn't you, Spock?"

The science officer turned his cool gaze to the doctor. "In fact, after several hours of work, I was able to salvage only two words from the corrupted chip . . . though I do appreciate your high estimation of my skills, Dr. McCoy."

Before he could respond—a sentiment along the lines of don't-flatter-yourself—the captain stepped in, steering them back on track.

"The two words are 'from thirty-one,' " Jim said, looking at each of them in turn. "Does that seem familiar to anyone? Think carefully, it could be important."

McCoy gave it a few seconds before shaking his

head. He supposed he could come up with something given time, but it didn't ring any bells.

"It could mean anything," Sulu said, expressing exactly what McCoy was thinking. Scott and Uhura both nodded.

"As I've already told the captain, the computer listed one hundred seventy-one thousand, nine hundred and forty-two references to the number thirty-one, not including stardates," Spock said. McCoy opened his mouth to ask if Spock meant the ship's computer or his own brain when Jim intervened yet again.

"As all of you know, there are a number of questions regarding the *Sphinx* that we don't have answers to," he said firmly. "The unidentified man on the bridge, Mr. Scott's discovery of the graviton field, how she ended up a runaway in the first place—and now this. The answers are out there, somewhere—but as much as I want to find them, I received a text message from Starfleet less than an hour ago, a response to our 1500 report regarding the thirty-eighth passenger and the possible cloak connection . . . telling me that they would be appointing another investigation team."

McCoy frowned, exchanging a confused look with Scotty, who shook his head in disbelief. It explained Jim's obvious discontent.

"That doesn't make any sense. Did they say why, Captain?" the engineer asked.

"No, but as soon as this meeting is over, I'm going to find out—a private communication link with the closest HQ station, so I can hear it for myself," Jim said, nodding at Uhura. "And since it appears I'm going to have to sell them on the idea of letting us continue, I was hoping one of you might recognize the 'thirty-one' reference. Anything I can use to convince them would be helpful, since our good record doesn't seem to be enough."

The captain controlled himself well, but the anger was there, barely hidden. McCoy knew from experience that Jim had already heavily invested himself in solving the mysterious tragedy—not necessarily his healthiest trait, getting emotionally involved so quickly, but it was also one of the things that made him an inspired captain.

There were a few guesses as to what "thirty-one" might mean, a brief update from each department, and the meeting was over. Jim said he'd let everyone know Starfleet's final decision as soon as he heard it, and excused himself from the room with a curt nod. Uhura left with him, shooting an uncertain glance back at the rest of them as they stood up from the table.

"What's this all about, Mr. Spock, do you have an idea?" Scotty asked worriedly.

Spock hesitated before speaking. "I wouldn't care to speculate at this juncture, Mr. Scott."

"In other words, no," McCoy jabbed, but his heart wasn't in it. He still felt tired. The one consolation was that Spock seemed even less inclined to go the rounds.

"Gentlemen," Spock said, and left without another word. Sulu shrugged at them and quickly followed.

"Care for a bit of dinner, Doctor?" Scott asked, but McCoy shook his head, wiggling his sore toes.

"Actually, I think I'm going to go soak my feet,"

he said, and smiled a little. He was off-duty until morning, and all he had to look forward to for the next several days was logging patient numbers and test results for a large group of basically healthy people. He abruptly decided that his own physical results could wait until he got a good night's sleep.

"I think I'm finally starting to figure out that I'm not as young as I used to be, Mr. Scott."

Scotty smiled ruefully. "Aye; ain't it a bugger?"

He asked Lieutenant Uhura to connect him with the nearest command base, only a sector away, and pipe it straight to the private office closest to the bridge. It had occurred to him that security considerations might have played a part in Starfleet's decision not to use the *Enterprise,* perhaps something they would reveal to him on a secured line.

Kirk stood next to the office's small wall screen, his arms crossed as he waited for Uhura. The room was cool and seemed obnoxiously bright, though he knew his anger and impatience tended to make him irritable and hypersensitive, another fine combination of emotions. Starfleet didn't want them to conduct the investigation? Fine—but he'd know why, he deserved as much after the hoops they'd jumped through to save the *Sphinx.*

Through the speaker beneath the screen, Uhura informed him that a Commodore Jefferson had been reached at Starbase 27, and that the connection was being relayed through a DS transmitter. Kirk thanked her and dropped his arms as he turned to face the screen, not wanting to come across as overly confrontational before hearing the whole story.

There was a toneless stutter of sound and the blank screen became a picture, the head and shoulders of a distinguished older man, his silvering hair slicked back from a well-lined brow, a friendly expression on his tanned face.

"Captain Kirk, I presume," he said, in a light voice that matched his polished demeanor. "Carl Jefferson. It's a pleasure to meet you, though you'll forgive me if I don't shake hands."

Surprised, Kirk smiled, in spite of his intentions. He hadn't heard that one before. "The pleasure's mine, sir. You'll forgive me if I come straight to the point, Commodore—have you been apprised of our current situation?"

Jefferson nodded. "I believe so, Captain. We received a copy of your report filed, ah, 5462.1, 1500 hours, from Starfleet Command, and their response. You've been asked to continue on to your next destination, Deep Space Station M-20, with the *U.S.S. Sphinx* in tow. There will be an inquest team waiting to receive the ship, though I don't know who has been officially appointed to lead the investigation, not at present. Does that describe your current situation?"

"Yes, sir," Kirk said, studying the man's open, pleasant face, withholding judgment for the moment on his sincerity.

"Is there a problem, Captain? Were the orders unclear?"

"The orders were clear, sir, but not the reason for them," Kirk said, throwing as much diplomatic charm as he could into the words. "We have the ship with us . . . and having already begun an exploration into the loss of the crew, and the near-destruction of the ship itself, I'm wondering why we haven't been asked to continue."

Jefferson sighed. "Of course. I'd wonder the same thing, in your position. I hope you understand, it's not a question of your competence, or the abilities of your crew. . . . Captain, did you know Jack Casden?"

"No, but I've read his file," Kirk said. "Several commendations, a solid record . . . he appeared to be well thought of as an officer."

"He was, throughout most of his career," Jefferson said. "Nine years since his first command. But what wasn't noted in his file were his political leanings. Captain Casden was a strong proponent of the Federation making peace with its enemies, Romulans and Klingons, among others. Practically an activist. He thought the Federation should disarm, to set the example of pacifism and nonviolent confrontation."

Kirk frowned, crossing his arms. "I don't know that I agree with his proposal, but it's a noble sentiment. There are a number of Federation societies that oppose the use of force, except in the most extreme circumstances."

"And if it was just a sentiment, I'd agree completely," Jefferson said. "But for Casden, it was more than that. It appears that he may have been in unauthorized contact with the Romulans. About two weeks ago, HQ Admin was running a routine check of stored computer logs from a number of starships—and someone noticed that some of the *Sphinx*'s assignment reports had been tampered with. A more intensive search turned up computer evidence that over the past two years, the *Sphinx* has made three separate excursions into the Neutral Zone, from the Lantaru sector."

"Computer records aren't that difficult to falsify," Kirk said slowly. An image of Ben Finney flashed through his mind and was gone, leaving a whisper of sorrow in its wake.

"No . . . but three days ago, just as an investigation into Casden's activities was being put together, the *Sphinx* disappeared," Jefferson said, his expression grim. "No contact at all until you found them—"

"—coming out of the Lantaru sector," Kirk said, all the pieces falling into place. A meeting with the Romulans would explain the graviton field . . .

. . . *and the unidentified man could have been a spy for the Romulans.* Maybe they decided they didn't want Casden around anymore. Or maybe Casden decided he couldn't live with the depth of guilt that his treasonous behavior had inspired, and decided to take his Romulan contact down with him.

Along with his crew? No, it had to be the Romulans . . . except how did he get his own men to go along with crossing into the Neutral Zone, not once but three times?

"The unknown person you discovered was undoubtedly Casden's contact," Jefferson continued. "And as for the graviton reading, it's simply not possible that the *Sphinx* came about it innocently. Starfleet Intelligence has just opened a research facility to study cloaking technology, but that's on one of Neptune's moons. Nereid, I believe."

The commodore was apparently unaware of the *Enterprise*'s involvement in obtaining the Federation's only cloaking device, though Kirk wasn't surprised. The assignment had been highly classified . . .

. . . and maybe that's how Casden explained it to his crew—a secret Intelligence mission. If they trusted him, they might have gone along with it.

"So. As I'm sure you now understand, Starfleet is planning a thorough investigation into all of this, one that could take weeks or even months to complete," Jefferson said. "As I said before, your qualifications to handle the inquiry are not in doubt—rather, it's a matter of time and resources."

"I understand," Kirk said, "and I appreciate your candor, Commodore. I'll send our final summary along to Starfleet Command."

"Fine, that's fine," Jefferson said smoothly, smiling. "Was there anything else, Captain Kirk?"

"Actually, there is. My first officer found a data chip that apparently belonged to the unidentified passenger—"

"Oh?" Jefferson sat up straighter, his smile fading. "That wasn't mentioned in your report. Is there anything on it?"

The commodore's casual, friendly air suddenly seemed forced, and for a half second, Kirk felt a tiny stir of doubt—but it was gone just as quickly. The news about Casden's seditious activities had obviously affected him, making him unaccountably paranoid. Jefferson was a Starfleet commodore, for God's sake.

"Not really," Kirk said. "The chip was badly damaged, what we did get could mean anything—two words, 'from thirty-one.' "

The commodore shook his head, his smile returning. "You're right, that could mean anything. Well. It's been a pleasure meeting you, Captain, but I'm afraid I have some other business to attend to. . . ."

"Of course," Kirk said. "Thank you for your time, Commodore."

Jefferson leaned forward, reaching toward the screen, and the picture dissolved. Kirk stood for another moment, thinking about Jack Casden, about pacifistic zeal carried too far. The ideals of peace were worth working toward, certainly, but reality wasn't ideal . . . something that Casden hadn't discovered until it was too late.

The road to hell . . . It was sad, but it made him angry, too. Regardless of politics, right or wrong, a captain was responsible for the lives of his crew. Leaders had to hold themselves to a higher standard than most; men made mistakes, and a man who led others had to do better than that, even if that sometimes meant denying his own humanity.

Like R. M. Merrick. Or Garth of Izar . . . or Ron Tracey, or Matt Decker—

He frowned, dismissing the disturbing train of thought, not liking where it was headed. They had a science conference to get to. Kirk headed for the bridge, turning his focus to ship's business—but try as he might, his focus kept wandering back to the reality of Jack Casden and how common it was, that well-meaning people could become so very lost.

Chapter Five

From a deep and peaceful place of being, Spock allowed his consciousness to rise, observing the changes within as the colorless layers fell away. No awareness, then his own deep breathing, his heartbeat and the sensation of returning from abstract to form; no time or activity, then an understanding of movement and acknowledgment of the inevitable.

Alone in his quarters, Spock remained just below the surface of his individual reality, allowing streams of unmolded thought and feeling to enter his mind. Thoughts and feelings that he would note but not participate in, observe and let pass. This simple meditation was taught to Vulcan children, a part of the training process that most discarded before reaching physical maturity . . . but because of his mixed parentage, Spock regularly included the meditation as part of his morning study.

In the seventeen hours since Mr. Scott's announcement of the cloak-specific graviton field around the *Sphinx,* Spock had reflected on the *Enterprise*'s mission to obtain the Romulan cloaking device multiple times. The connection of recent past to present was certainly understandable, there being the common element of the cloaking device . . . but his memories of the Romulan commander, and his inability to entirely suppress those memories, was the reason for this morning's observance meditation. It had been weeks since he'd considered her, but his belief that he had excised her from his deeper self had been in error.

Thought without form, feeling transformed into thought. The sound of her voice. He remembered, recalling the physical sensations when she had whispered her name in his ear. The powerful lilt of promise beneath her words. The internal discord aroused when she'd questioned his betrayal, pain and anger roughening her inflection, pain and anger that he had caused.

Observed and released. The touch of her hand. Inflamed senses, and a creation of conflict by physical contact. The creation of hunger, of wistfulness, her own emanations feeding his—and his private displeasure. Knowing what the immediate future held, the knowledge robbing him of a full connection to her; the displeasure of knowing that he had allowed the erosion of his discipline . . . and the acceptance that at the time, at the shock of her warm fingers against his, he had not cared.

Thoughts moving past him, away from him. The final understanding of the disharmonious duality— that he had achieved success through the manipulation of an officer of the Romulan Empire . . . and had wounded a woman who'd made herself vulnerable to him. The final personal outcome, that both of them had returned to the comforts of individual and cultural identity, finding solace in the self-assigned roles each had chosen long before their meeting. She was probably back with her people by now, presumably having branded their interaction a mistake.

Observed. Excised, surely. To maintain the Vulcan discipline, to truly control oneself as an extension of intellect rather than emotion, it was often necessary to recognize the existence of the alternative. Because of who and what he was, it would likely always take some effort to recognize emotion without yielding to it . . . and judging himself harshly for his failures was an emotional indulgence in and of itself. He must observe and learn, recognize and allow to pass.

The difficulty he encountered when considering the Romulan commander and the theft of the cloaking device was that he could find no rationalization for his emotional or intellectual behavior—nor could he rationalize Starfleet's involvement in such blatant espionage. As officers of Starfleet, he and the captain had been following orders, orders to deceive and to steal, justified by the promise of an end that would outweigh the means. Their objective had been met, but he couldn't support Starfleet's choice to employ such treacherous methods . . . and he couldn't convince himself that he'd had no options, regardless of his commitments and loyalties. There were always options.

Enough.

He had considered all of the key elements; at pres-

ent, further contemplation would likely prove inef-
fectual.

Spock closed the meditation, releasing the
thoughts and restating the essence of his discipline
before taking the last step back to full awareness. He
opened his eyes and was again connected to himself
as Spock, a man of science and of strict self-control,
first officer of the *Enterprise*.

His shift began in less than an hour. Spock rose
from his knees and went to prepare.

Although Christine Chapel arrived early for her
shift, Dr. McCoy had beaten her there. The doctor
was sitting at his desk, a stack of file disks in front
of him, staring at the computer screen with a perfectly blank expression. And since he wasn't scheduled to come on until half an hour after her shift
began—and was notoriously grumpy first thing in
the morning, besides, which was why he was never
early—she immediately assumed the worst.

He found something. One of the physicals.

"Doctor?"

He didn't seem to hear her. Christine took a few
hesitant steps toward him, increasingly disturbed by
that blank expression. He seemed pale, too.

"Dr. McCoy," she said, her voice made strong by
concern as she walked quickly to his side. He finally
looked up just as she reached him—and she saw that
the computer screen wasn't even turned on.

"Hello, Christine," he said mildly, unsmiling, his
eyes dazed and distant, and her worry escalated into
fear. The doctor *never* looked like that.

"What is it? What's wrong?"

McCoy blinked, his gaze refocusing—and then scowled at her, the familiar expression instantly lifting a weight off her chest.

"What do you mean, what's wrong?" he grumbled. "It's morning, that's what's wrong."

"I'm sorry," she said, smiling in relief, inwardly calling herself all kinds of fool. A real goose, her grandmother would have said. "You just seemed so far away for a moment, and when I saw the files, I thought—well, never mind what I thought."

The doctor cocked an eyebrow at her. "You saw the files and thought . . .?"

She hesitated, not sure if he actually wanted to know or if he was just looking for something to tease her about. Probably both—except he still seemed pale, his expression strangely unguarded.

"I thought maybe you were upset by something you saw in the physical results from yesterday," she said uncertainly. "I was planning on looking them over before you came in . . . *did* you find something wrong, Doctor?"

McCoy stood up as she spoke, answering her over his shoulder as he walked across the room, a laugh in his voice. "Are you kidding? I'm surprised we're still in business."

That's not an answer. Something *was* wrong, she could feel it, and it wasn't like him at all to be so evasive with her—

Christine had a sudden and terrible thought, too terrible to keep inside.

"Have you looked at my test results?" she asked, the hollow, carefully neutral sound of her own voice giving her a chill.

McCoy had stopped at the far counter and was digging through a drawer for something. At her question, he looked up—and whatever he saw on her face made him smile and shake his head, his eyes sparkling with good humor.

"Yes, and I'm sorry to tell you this, Nurse, but you've lost weight."

"Oh?" Inside, she jumped up and down, clapping her hands; all those salads were finally paying off. "Well, that's—that's fine."

"I'm sure it is," he said, smirking, and came up with a couple of food cards before closing the drawer. "And since I don't officially start work for another half hour, I think I'm going to celebrate with a nice, fat breakfast. Eggs, bacon, the works."

"If you can afford that, I guess I'm not the only one who's lost a little weight," she said jokingly.

"I guess not." Dr. McCoy's smirk faded, and she realized that he just looked tired.

Of course he's tired, he's not a morning person and he was probably half asleep when I came in . . .

"I'll be back in time for my shift," he said. "Miss Eckert is first today, is that right?"

Christine nodded. "Yes, Doctor."

"Fine. If she comes in early, just . . . just tell her to wait."

He turned and walked out of sickbay, not looking back. She stared after him for a few seconds and then shook her head, deciding that she was reading too much into his slightly odd behavior. Everyone had an off day, now and again; she really *could* be a goose sometimes . . .

. . . but not a fat goose, she thought, smiling as she patted her skirt over her hips.

Christine sat down in front of the computer and called up the day's schedule, humming to herself as she started plugging in file disks and scanning results. She didn't notice that Dr. McCoy's file wasn't in the stack, and by the time he returned from breakfast, he was his old self again.

Christine had caught him off guard, arriving only moments after he'd read the test results, but McCoy had done the best he could to cover. He didn't have breakfast, aimlessly walking the corridors until it was time for him to go back, thinking of nothing at all. Shock, he supposed.

The morning went by in a haze, though he put some effort into acting out business as usual—a few jokes told, a few stories passed on to the changing parade of faces. He thought he did very well, considering. He wasn't sure what to think, what to do, but he'd seen the worry in his nurse's face and knew absolutely that any more of it—from anyone—would be too painful to bear.

McCoy forced himself to eat a few bites of tasteless chicken at lunch, not because he was hungry but because there was work to be done and he didn't particularly want to collapse. He had weeks, maybe even months before the symptoms would begin to interfere with his work; he saw no point in announcing it to the world by passing out from malnutrition.

The afternoon went well; he actually managed not to think about the diagnosis for a few hours, and even laughed out loud at one of M'Benga's stories when the doctor arrived for the evening shift. The denial didn't last, though; he could feel the truth bearing down on him, seeking acceptance. Not wanting to bother with dinner, McCoy grabbed a handful of meal supplements on his way out and went straight to his quarters.

A few pills washed down with a glass of stale water, sitting on the edge of his bed. Dr. McCoy pulled off his boots and lay down, lacing his fingers over his chest and closing his eyes. Only then, safely alone and without responsibility, did he allow himself to think about the results from his physical.

Xenopolycythemia. Terminal. Over the years he'd learned about hundreds upon hundreds of diseases, so many that often they blurred together, but the rare blood disorder was one of the clear ones. It was the name, xenopolycythemia. It rolled off the tongue, like the name of some exotic flower or faraway place.

The disease process wasn't nearly so enchanting, though just as memorable. The disorder caused an enlargement of the spleen, along with a serious overproduction of blood cells, red and white. Caught in its earliest stages—for him, about three months ago—the spleen could be removed, with a solid prognosis for full recovery. Once it insinuated itself into the lymphatic system, however, it would spread to the lymph nodes and other more vulnerable organs. And that was the beginning of the end.

Already too late for me, he thought, wondering when the sadness would hit, the fear . . . he felt numb and tired. Maybe sorry the way one felt upon hearing about somebody else's tragedy, what-a-shame, but nothing more. He didn't know if that was good or not.

The course of the disease was simple enough. Slowly, very slowly, the increased blood-cell count would take its toll. Pain in the extremities, weakness and fatigue as his heart worked to pump the increasingly viscous blood. In the last few months, he would be bedridden, his every exertion putting strain on the overworked muscle. By then, enlarged mediastinal lymph nodes would be putting serious extrinsic pressure on his heart, making it have to work even harder . . . until it simply gave out. He had a year at most.

What would he leave behind? A few friends, but no family. He hadn't been serious with a woman since Nancy, and she was long gone; there'd be no one to remember him and weep for a lost love. A good service record, and perhaps a mention in some future medical text for this technique or that—another random old name glossed over by a bright-eyed young med student, who wouldn't know or care that Leonard McCoy had been a man with a life, a man who had seen many things, who had been in love and been alone, who had died before his forty-second birthday from a terminal disease.

There were no tears, but the ache of his poor heart followed him into sleep, sending him haunted dreams of every patient he'd ever lost, their drawn, mute faces and glassy eyes seeking him out as one of their own.

Chapter Six

Captain's Log, Stardate 5465.4:

We'll be arriving at Station M-20 within the hour, where we are expected to turn over the U.S.S. Sphinx *to a specially appointed task force—one which has presumably already begun their investigation into the alleged treason of Starfleet Captain Jack Casden. A small memorial service is also planned for the* Sphinx's *lost crew.*

Because towing the Sphinx *required that we travel at low warp speeds, we have already missed a full day of the Federation's four-day science summit. Owing to security considerations, there will be no ship leave for R-and-R purposes; however, a number of crew members from the* Enterprise's *science and engineering divisions have requested special dispensation to attend some of the conference's open de-*

bates, which I am more than willing to approve.

Spock was waiting in the transporter room when Kirk arrived, and Mr. Scott was at the controls. The summit's panels had finished for the day, but a representative of the investigation team was supposed to be waiting to meet with them. Although he now understood the reason for Starfleet's decision, Kirk wanted to be absolutely sure that he was releasing the *Sphinx*—and the information his crew had uncovered—into capable hands.

Maybe then, I'll actually be able to let it go. . . .

He hadn't been able to shake the uneasiness that Casden's apparent breakdown had inspired; if anything, it was getting worse. How often had he seen good men, admirable men, tragically crushed beneath the weight of their responsibilities? What if—

Stop it, he commanded himself—and as always, felt a faint glimmer of surprise when it actually worked.

Kirk walked straight to the platform, Spock following.

"The doctor won't be joining us?" Spock asked.

"No, he said he had too much work to catch up on," Kirk said, turning his attention to the engineer. "Mr. Scott, I assume you'll be attending tomorrow's discussion on ways to artificially enhance dilithium?"

"Aye, and looking forward to it, sir, me and the lads," Scott answered, suddenly positively beaming. Kirk could actually see Scotty warming up to the topic and quickly headed him off, smiling inwardly at his engineer's enthusiasm; he was pleased and proud that so many of his crew had asked to attend parts of the summit.

"Energize," Kirk said, straightening his shoulders.

A sparkle of light later, he and Mr. Spock were standing on another platform in a much larger room, its decor entirely utilitarian. Kirk reflexively assessed the new environment, taking it in at a glance before focusing his attention on the man standing a few meters in front of them, command yellow, gray hair, and a wide smile—

"Captain James Tiberius Kirk," he thundered, walking forward with his hand out.

Kirk grinned, stepping down from the platform and extending his own. They shook firmly, Kirk making the introduction.

"Mr. Spock, Captain Gage Darres, one of Starfleet's finest. Captain, my first officer, Mr. Spock."

Spock bowed his head. "A pleasure, sir."

Darres's eyes were sparkling. "I've heard good things about you, Mr. Spock—but I have to ask, what's a logical fellow like yourself doing, hanging around a man like Kirk?"

Knowing that Spock would probably try to answer, Kirk quickly interceded on his friend's behalf. "Ignore him, Spock. The captain is getting on in years, he doesn't know what he's saying."

Darres laughed. Spock wisely elected not to say anything.

"Let me buy you two a drink," Darres said, motioning toward the doors. "I've got a bottle of semidecent Saurian brandy in my quarters, we can talk there. It'll be a lot quieter than any of the station's bars, what with the summit and all . . . you wouldn't believe how much some of those science people can put down—"

"Actually, we have some business to attend to first," Kirk started, but Darres interrupted him.

"I know," he said, his smile dropping away. "I was tapped yesterday to lead the investigation. Come on, I'm not far from here."

So much for worrying about the investigation. Casden's actions *had* been weighing heavily on his mind, reminding him of past events he wanted to stay in the past . . . but he'd also been concerned about bowing out of the situation, leaving it to somebody else. Gage Darres, though—he couldn't think of anyone more qualified to handle it.

They left the transporter room, Darres leading the way. It was good to see him again; it had been years since their last meeting. They'd served together on the *U.S.S. Farragut,* when Kirk was still a lieutenant and Darres had just made commander. Darres had been assigned to the ship from Starfleet Intelligence after the incident on Tycho IV, and had seen Kirk through a fairly dark period of his life, even talking him out of resigning at one point. Although they'd only worked together for about six months, Kirk had looked up to him—and in fact still felt a measure of pride when he thought about it, that Darres had singled him out as someone to encourage.

M-20 was a huge station, the standard DS design of multiple modules connected by rays, but much larger than most. It was capable of holding fifty-five hundred people, in fact, but he wouldn't have known it from how crowded the corridors were; dozens of people pushed past each other, congregations form- ing and unforming, blocking foot traffic at every turn. They passed mostly humans, Starfleet and civilian wearing coded identity badges showing them to be guests of the conference . . . but Kirk saw more than a few representatives from other Federa- tion and Federation-friendly planets. There were a number of Vulcans, most of whom took note of Spock, nodding politely in his direction. Kirk also saw a trio of fully suited Regulans, a Halkan, a handful of Tellarites, even a few beings he didn't im- mediately recognize . . . it was a diverse group, to say the least.

And loud.

"I thought there were only supposed to be about seven or eight hundred people attending," Kirk said, raising his voice slightly to be heard over a number of conversations.

"There are," Darres answered. "But they're all bunking in this area. Two days ago, Mr. Miatsu— he's the station manager—had the bright idea to put a few of the more renowned Federation docs up in officers' quarters, on the other side of the station. We were asked to volunteer as gentlemen, you know the drill. Anyway, I'm here for the duration of the sum- mit."

A bit farther down the corridor, Darres stopped in front of a door, tapping his identification number into a lock panel. The three of them entered, the din from the hall cut to a low murmur as the door shut behind them.

The guest rooms were generic and unadorned, but

nice. Darres motioned them toward a plush sitting area, scooping up two glasses and the distinctive brandy bottle from a counter after Spock declined his repeated drink offer. The three men sat, Darres pouring for himself and Kirk.

Darres held up his glass, unsmiling. "To the crew of the *Sphinx*," he said solemnly, and drank. Kirk nodded his agreement and followed suit, the brandy warm and smooth going down.

There was a brief silence, Kirk studying Darres's face as the captain poured himself another. A few more lines, his hair completely gray now, but he still carried himself with the kind of strength and vitality that Kirk had always admired, had worked hard to project in his own command. Darres motioned to Kirk's glass, but Kirk shook his head.

"It's good to see you again, Captain," Kirk said, smiling. "And I have to say, I'm glad that you'll be the one handling the investigation. Mr. Spock has compiled a complete index of everything we found for your team, all the medical reports, inspection files, you name it. Has Starfleet already sent you the doctored logs?"

Darres nodded slowly, sitting back in his chair with his untouched second drink. "They have."

When he didn't expand on the topic, Kirk didn't press any further, understanding that Darres might have been instructed not to discuss the investigation . . . but just as he was about to change the subject to something a little more insubstantial, Darres abruptly volunteered his thoughts in no uncertain terms, changing everything.

"I knew Jack, and he was as loyal to the Federation as the day is long," Darres said. "It's a setup, Jim, the whole thing, but I'll be damned if I know why."

After his decidedly singular statement, Darres swallowed the contents of his glass and stared down into the empty container, expressionless. Spock was intrigued by his supposition. When the captain didn't immediately respond, only watching Darres with a look of surprise, Spock took it upon himself to ask a question of his own.

"May I ask upon what grounds you make this claim, sir?"

Darres smiled faintly, without humor. "Background, his and mine. Jack Casden and I both worked for Starfleet Intelligence HQ around the same time, about thirteen years ago. I was shuffling papers for admin, he was looking at a field command, but we were in the same building for about two years. We got to be pretty good friends."

Captain Kirk's response was gentle. "A lot can happen in thirteen years. People change."

Darres leaned forward, looking intently at the captain. "I agree. But about five years ago, we both ended up docked at the same station, pure coincidence. We had dinner, a few drinks . . . and fundamentally, he hadn't changed at all.

"It's been a few years since you and I last met up, but we used to know each other fairly well," Darres continued. "What if someone told you that I now believe Klingons are good guys? That we should go ahead and hand over one of our starships for them to study, so that they could see we had honorable intentions . . . would you believe it?"

"That's not the same thing, Gage—"

Darres was insistent. "Humor me."

The captain hesitated, then shook his head. "No. No, I wouldn't," he said softly.

"I *knew* him, Jim," Darres said, most vehemently. "Sure, he wanted peace with our enemies, but he wasn't stupid, he knew that trust takes time, he never would have supported a full Starfleet disarmament . . . and there's no way in hell he would have contacted the Romulans on his own. I'm telling you, Jack Casden would have laid his life down to protect the Federation's interests."

Spock could see that Darres had made his point with the captain, but he hadn't yet touched on the primary base of his essentially emotional argument. The captain had apparently deduced the same.

"If you're right about this, who would want to frame him?" he asked. "And why?"

"There's also the question of how," Spock added. "Your belief in his innocence requires a conspiracy—the fabrication of a ship's records, the creation of or the explanation for the graviton field . . . and if he was not in the Lantaru sector by his own volition, who ordered him there, and where is the record of it?"

Darres shook his head, his intensity changing direction. "I don't know, but I'm going to find out. Believe me, whoever did this is going to be very sorry that I was picked to lead the investigation."

The captain was watching him closely. "And if you uncover evidence that Casden was involved?"

"I'm after the truth, Jim," Darres said. "If I'm wrong about him, I'm wrong."

The captain seemed satisfied with his answer. "All right. The *Sphinx* is still in our tractor—I assume you've got someone standing by for the transfer?"

At Darres's nod, the captain continued, rising to his feet. Spock did the same. "Tell them to talk to my chief engineer, Mr. Scott . . . Mr. Spock, the files?"

Spock handed the data chip he'd been holding to Captain Darres, who also stood.

"I want to get my team started on this tonight, but maybe we can meet for lunch tomorrow, or dinner?" Darres asked. "I'd like to have a chance to talk, catch up a little."

Darres nodded at Spock. "You should come, too. I'll fill you in on a few of his old skeletons, and you can fill me in on the new ones."

Discussing the captain's flaws in front of him did not sound even slightly appealing, and Spock expected to be attending panels all day. Not wanting to be impolite, he inclined his head, a noncommittal acknowledgment of the offer.

The three of them moved toward the door, the captain and Darres walking in front of him.

"Can you keep me apprised of any new developments?" the captain asked.

Darres nodded. "Technically, I was ordered not to talk to anyone on the *station*," he said. "But if you're on your ship . . ."

The captain smiled. "Good."

Spock was somewhat surprised that both men would decide to interpret the order literally, but if it was as Darres said, it was not improper—and with his own curiosity raised, Spock was not sure he would have commented on it either way. One of the many things that serving under Captain Kirk had taught him was that finding one's way around a directive sometimes created the most expeditious path to one's objective. Or, as the captain himself had once clearly stated, there was nothing wrong with bending the rules every now and then to get where you needed to go.

Jain Suni rose early on the second day of the summit, had a light breakfast, then spent an hour or so jotting down notes for Bendes's evening panel. She was already bored with the conference, uninterested in the decidedly dull company of their peers. True, many were brilliant, but she had yet to hear a truly original idea . . . or to meet a scientist with a vibrant, exciting personality and a good sense of humor. Suni knew they existed, but apparently none had opted to attend the Federation summit. And unfortunately for her, Bendes absolutely insisted that they give it at least another day.

And what Bendes wants . . . She didn't bother to finish the cliché as she stored her notes—notes that he probably wouldn't end up using, anyway—even wearied by her own thoughts on the matter. She felt herself to be a woman of action rather than talk, which made the summit a distraction, unimportant. Most of the people speaking had already published their ideas, and she was a voracious reader . . . but unlike her, Bendes enjoyed the politics, and believed that an open exchange created open-mindedness.

The man was strangely idealistic in his own way, but Suni was determined to be supportive if it killed her . . . and besides, there was currently nothing for either of them to do back at the lab, and if there was anything worse than being bored, it was having to wait patiently for results.

After a few exercises and a shower, Suni dressed for the day, deliberately choosing a low-cut, formfitting bodysuit of dark green, that looked see-through sheer but wasn't. Most of her colleagues would be shocked, envious, or deeply interested, depending on species and persuasion . . . and she had to admit, she enjoyed the overall antilogy factor. Quantum-field theoreticians weren't generally expected to be extroverts.

A quick look over the conference schedule, and she decided that Bendes was most likely to be sitting in on one of the subspace theory discussions—what forms of natural energy might exist in certain strata of subspace and how to get at them, definitely old news. She'd already read the key speaker's less than plausible—and entirely tedious—speculations on the matter, but thought she might as well touch base with Bendes, see if he'd heard from the lab. She also wanted to offer up her notes for his future-of-technology discussion. He and five other Starfleet giants would be speaking in the largest of the assembly rooms, the turnout expected to be high . . . and without guidance, a few stabilizing facts to refer to, Bendes tended to stray. Passionately.

After tucking a few essentials into a small pack on her belt, Suni left her quarters and headed for the subspace discussion, drawing a number of looks along the way. Even the Vulcans she passed looked, although their reactions were obviously internal, not a trace of interest on the outside. She liked Vulcans, they had a decent, life-affirming culture and well-trained minds . . . but having debated a few back in school, it had finally become apparent to her that they didn't seem to count feelings of superiority as emotion, which she considered cheating. She didn't know that it was true of all Vulcans, but certainly those she'd met.

She walked through the security gate, and had just reached the conference room she wanted when the door opened and a Starfleet officer backed out, in command uniform. He looked familiar, though she could only see part of his profile—young, human, medium tall with broad shoulders. She was interested already, and when he turned around, she found herself grinning. Captain James Kirk, of the *Enterprise*. She'd only met him once, for just a moment or two at a crowded party . . . five, six years ago? He'd made an impression, though; she'd recognize that handsome face anywhere. And whether or not he remembered her, she suddenly suspected that it might be her turn to make an impression.

"James Kirk," she said, stepping forward, glad she'd decided on the bodysuit by the way he looked at her—gallant, courteous, but with a sparkle in his eye that wouldn't have been there if she'd worn something else.

"I'm sorry," he said, smiling boyishly as he shook her hand. "Have we met?"

"Five years ago, I believe. On Earth. We were both at a dinner party, honoring David Kincaid's retirement from the Academy. He taught physics."

"You're in Starfleet?" he asked, still smiling.

Suni shook her head. "No, I was one of his research assistants. He also taught relativistic quantum mechanics at New Northern Cal. I graded papers, mostly."

Kirk folded his arms, frowning slightly but not seriously.

"Are you going to put me out of my misery, or are you actually going to make me guess your name?"

As charming as she remembered. "Jain. Dr. Jain Suni, in fact," she said, looking into his eyes. They were warm, friendly—and definitely interested. She felt like laughing, the coincidence of meeting up with him again as unexpected as the sudden attraction . . . his and her own.

Kirk started to say something else, then stopped and glanced back at the conference room before starting again. "You know, it's a little embarrassing to admit, but I was having trouble following the discussion in there. My physics terminology is somewhat outdated. If you're not too busy, perhaps you wouldn't mind giving me a quick remedial course . . . ? I'd spring for the coffee."

Not particularly subtle, but she'd always preferred a direct approach . . . and there was a sweetness to him that was very appealing, very honest. Bendes didn't actually *need* her for anything, he could use his communicator if he did. And she certainly wasn't interested in yawning her way through another day of circular reasoning, just killing time until they could get back to the lab. . . .

"Captain, I'd like that very much," she said, and when he offered his arm, she gladly took it, the possibilities for her day not seeming quite so dull, after all.

Chapter Seven

McCoy avoided thinking about it. In the first three days following his diagnosis, he evaded all but the most superficial contact, even managing to beg off seeing Jim by claiming too much work—which wasn't actually a lie, since he threw himself into running the physicals, arriving before and staying long after each shift. He thought about everyone else's test results, he thought about recalibrating his instruments and increasing crew efficiency and putting new cabinets up behind his desk. When he wasn't thinking about any of those things, McCoy slept, finding himself suddenly exhausted at the end of each workday, half asleep before he hit the sack each night.

It was most commonly referred to as denial, and he was more than happy to wait it out; he'd have plenty of time to wallow in the awareness of his mortality when he was stuck in bed a few months down the line. A lot of people seemed to think denial was a bad thing, but he knew from experience that the human mind could only deal with some issues when it damn well felt like it, and not a moment sooner—and he, for one, was not going to rush headlong into some emotional abyss until he had to. But early on the morning of the fourth day, the *Enterprise's* first full day at M-20, McCoy remembered Karen Patterson, and the denial gave way to hope.

It was an accident, really. Several of his lab staff had gone to the summit, which he'd used as an excuse to stay behind; Jim had pushed, cajoling, insisting that he needed someone to desert the conference with him, but McCoy had convinced him that he wasn't interested. The captain had been mildly annoyed, but had let it go after exacting a promise that McCoy would find time to beam over in the next day or so. The doctor had returned to work, only to realize that the summit had left him understaffed. He'd been so preoccupied with avoiding himself, he hadn't kept track of who he'd given leave to, nor had he bothered to make a note on the duty roster.

After a call to the lab confirmed it, the scowling doctor plopped himself in front of the computer, determined to get it worked out before the first crew members showed up for their scheduled exams.

"Computer, give me a list of medical division technicians who are currently not on duty, but who haven't signed out for ship leave," McCoy said. "Name only." Nurse West would be arriving in ten minutes, and he couldn't get at least one more person into the lab to rack samples; he'd have to get her to do it, which would earn him a solid week of disapproving looks and mumbled complaints. Sandra West was a competent assistant and usually as nice as pie, but she could raise holy hell if asked to do anything outside the scope of her duties.

"Working . . ." the computer clattered, the almost female voice sounding as emotionless as . . . well, as Spock.

"Carmen, Philip G.; Erickson, Alexander T.; Ivers, Carey N.; Peterson, Sarah T. . . ."

"Stop," McCoy said, frowning, picking through the line of syllables he'd heard, recognizing a name made up of two others.

Carey Peterson . . . Karen Patterson.

He abruptly stood up, remembering Karen, pacing the empty room as he dug for information. Med school, they'd had three or four classes together. Bright—genius-bright—red hair, terrible sense of humor. Pretty eyes. Her medical science had been impeccable, her diagnoses a hundred percent, but her bedside manner had been mediocre at best, cold fish at worst. She wasn't unfriendly, she was just one of those people who saw the disease rather than the patient. He vaguely remembered suggesting to her that she should consider focusing on surgery, something intricate and demanding that wouldn't require her to employ her people skills . . . and a few years after graduation, he'd received a note from her, saying that she'd moved into private research and was much happier.

He'd thought of her only a few times since, on every occasion because he'd been flipping through a Starfleet medical journal and run across her name. She'd published several times, authoring and coauthoring papers on rare human diseases, the material dense but brilliant, innovative, and if he remembered right . . .

"Computer, access medical library. Pull up every article or paper we've got with the name Karen Patterson on it . . ." Middle name, she'd had an unusual middle name . . . Mica? Nica?

"Karen Nico Patterson," he continued, astounded at the things one could remember when the need arose. "From those articles, cross-reference Patterson with the following words—xenopolycythemia, hematology, pathogenesis, disease."

"Working . . . seven articles found. Seven articles containing reference to disease. Seven articles containing reference to disease and hematology. Seven—"

"Are there any articles containing all of the words?" McCoy snapped; *ignorant machine.*

"Article published Stardate 2231.2 in Starfleet medical journal issue 421, written by Dr. Karen Nico Patterson. Article titled *Searching for Answers: Hope for Humans with Blood-Based Hyperplasia.*"

McCoy took a deep breath, then another. He'd remembered right. The article hadn't promised a cure, it had been about new research in the area—but xenopolycythemia was one form of blood-based hyperplasia.

"Computer, where is Dr. Patterson currently employed?"

Clatters and beeps. "Unknown."

"Where was she employed last, then?"

"Working . . . unable to find reference."

Dammit. "What's the last reference you have on file?"

"Dr. Karen Nico Patterson, passage booked to Lunar Colonies from Earth, Stardate 2716.6. Passage booked from Lunar Colonies to Altair VI, Stardate 2717.1."

Hardly two years ago. McCoy nodded to himself, his throat tight with urgency. "So she's on Altair VI."

"Negative. Current whereabouts of Karen Patterson unknown."

He clenched his fists, barely resisting an urge to break something. *Why didn't you just tell me that in the first place, you fool piece of—*

"Doctor, are you all right?"

Nurse West. McCoy turned to face her, wanting to throw her out, to find Karen, the thought that he hadn't found a replacement lab technician suddenly seeming ridiculously unimportant . . . but the slight, maternal frown on her face reminded him of where—and who—he was. Whatever his troubles, no matter how serious, he was CMO of the *Enterprise.* Until he was ready to bring in his shingle, he had responsibilities that he would not fail.

"It's this blasted computer," he growled, shaking his head. "Never mind, Nurse. The lab is short-staffed today, would you please call in Carmen or Peterson for a half shift?"

"Of course, Doctor."

As she bustled off to take care of it, McCoy walked to his desk and sat down, his feelings all tied up in knots. Remembering Karen Patterson's name and specialty had opened the door to hope—but it had also pushed him out of the calm, gray zone of denial, of feeling nothing at all.

No matter. If anyone alive can help me, it's Karen.

Now all he had to do was find her.

Jain Suni was amazing.

Coffee had become lunch, which had become a long, meandering walk around the station, the two of them laughing and talking like old friends in a matter of hours. She seemed to say whatever was on her mind, no matter how silly or pointed, not worrying at all about how she came across—and for Kirk, it was both refreshing and inspiring to be around such a confident young woman . . . particularly after last night's talk with Darres.

As much as he wanted to believe his old friend, there was no solid evidence to support his claim, and Spock had agreed. It still seemed most likely that Jack Casden was directly responsible for what had happened to his crew. Kirk had slept quite badly, worried about Darres, a semiconscious part of him deeply concerned that he might be watching another good man losing his way, a good man fooling himself by taking what he wanted to believe and calling it truth.

The outcome of his restless night was beginning his day moody and exhausted . . . and halfway through the first panel of the morning, one that had entirely absorbed Mr. Spock, he'd realized that he needed more coffee if he hoped to stay awake. Maybe a lot more.

And there she was. As though it was fated for us to meet.

Kirk had initially been interested by her looks, there was no denying it, and she *was* stunning— short, thick, dark hair framed her porcelain-fine face, her features strong and generous, her eyes incredibly bright. She was wearing some kind of clinging bodysuit that accentuated her curves, her softness, which he liked very much—but after spending time with her, he decided that her looks and figure were only accents, like physical expressions of her personality.

Not that I object to the package, he thought, watching her talk about the patterns she imagined in the stars outside the window, watching her trace the shapes on the glass with long fingers. They had stopped walking when they'd reached a mostly empty observation lounge at the end of the station's northernmost ray, choosing a small table in a semi-secluded corner of the room.

Kirk was intrigued and impressed by her, by everything about her. Jain had a great sense of humor, sharply witty without being cruel, her observations about her fellow scientists incredibly funny. She was smart but unpretentious about it, her comments on everything from Federation politics to time travel both thoughtful and interesting . . . and yet she somehow managed to reveal very little information about herself personally, her answers vague when he asked about her work or background.

A woman of mystery . . .

It had to be deliberate, a touch of artfulness for effect; she was only twenty-eight years old, a civilian working as a Starfleet consultant on some sort of research project. Whatever the reason for her mysterious behavior, it worked. Jain's playful evasions stirred his interest, making him want to know more about her.

". . . but I always thought it looked like—you're not listening, are you?"

Kirk smiled. "I'm afraid you caught me. I was thinking about something else."

Jain crossed her arms, a lovely smirk turning up one corner of her mouth. "Clever, Captain, but I see right through you."

"Tell me," he said, smiling wider.

"Now I'm supposed to ask you what you were thinking about, and you'll say something terribly flattering . . . at which point I'm so overwhelmed that I throw caution to the wind and melt into your arms, lost to the passion of the moment." She leaned back in her chair, looking quite satisfied with herself.

Kirk laughed. He hadn't felt so wonderfully challenged by a woman in a long time. "Would it have worked?"

"That depends on effort and quality," she answered. "For instance, if you had said something about how beautiful my eyes look in the starlight, absolutely not. Totally unoriginal, no effort at all, beyond having the nerve to say it."

"They do, you know," Kirk said. "Although I certainly would have tried harder than that."

Jain leaned forward, fixing him with her brilliant gaze as she rested her arms on the table. "All right, Jim," she said, her voice low, her smile slow and deliberate. "What were you thinking about?"

"Jain, I—"

A communicator chirped. Hers, not his.

"Talk about timing," Jain said casually, though he could tell she wasn't any happier about the interruption than he was. "I'm sorry, would you excuse me? This might take a minute."

"Of course," he said, standing as she got up from the table and stepped away, reaching into her belt for the offending device as she walked quickly across the room.

Kirk turned and looked out the window, not sure what he'd been about to say to her. The attraction was obviously mutual, but he'd also never met a woman more scrutinizing of his attentions . . . or less likely to be impressed by them. From what little time they'd spent together, he knew that she responded to honesty over idealism, to acknowledgments of vulnerability over projections of strength—

—but she wouldn't respect any man who tried to manipulate her emotions—and she would see it coming from light-years away.

Best not to try and impress her, or sit around worrying about what to say . . . or what was going to happen, for that matter. The truth of it was, she'd provided a wonderful diversion from how he'd been feeling, from the perplexed unhappiness that had been eating at him since the moment he'd set foot on the *Sphinx.* He hadn't even realized how absorbed he'd been with his own dark thoughts until she'd distracted him, just by being herself. As much as he wanted to touch her, to feel like she wanted him to—and the very thought made him want it even more—even if nothing at all happened, he was glad to have met her.

"What are you thinking about now, Captain?"

Jain slipped back into her chair before he could stand, watching him with an almost objective interest as he carefully considered her question. How to answer? He'd long ago recognized in himself a desire—almost a need—to feel truly connected to the women who attracted him. He met a woman he liked, he wanted to be with her, to feel close to her, and physical intimacy wasn't threatening in the same way that emotional intimacy could be—he had the terrible habit of making himself too vulnerable too fast, and it had cost him, time and again, something always pulling him away. Making love to a woman was the answer to his need for connection, to exchange something special without allowing room for hurt; he never lied or faked meaning, and because he honestly respected his partners, he never felt as though he'd used a woman selfishly . . . but there were times when he recognized the limitations to what could be shared in the bedroom, and wished for an even deeper connection. But to achieve it, he had to be willing to share more than just an hour or two of pleasure; he had to be willing to share himself, and that meant risking pain, for himself and for his partner—because in the end, they would always go their separate ways.

Jain simply watched him, as though recognizing that he was deciding how much of himself to risk . . . and it was that gentle understanding that helped him decide. He hardly knew her, but he believed in her, believed in what he saw—and what he saw was a mind and heart that didn't judge, a strong, smart woman who wanted only to know him a little better.

"I was thinking of how glad I am to have met you," he said, meeting her gaze directly. "Because I've had a hard time of it lately, I've been . . . *stuck*, I guess you could say. Caught someplace that I don't like very much. And today, meeting you . . ."

"You feel a little less stuck?" Jain asked, her expression open and empathetic.

"I do," he said, smiling a little.

"May I ask . . ." Jain hesitated, then started again. "If it's not too personal, may I ask about what's been troubling you? If you can't talk about it, or don't want to, I'll understand. But I'm interested."

If she'd asked in any other way, or offered help instead of curiosity, he wouldn't have felt comfortable answering. Her careful but direct approach was relaxing, though, almost as if she knew exactly what to say to put him at ease.

Kirk paused for a moment, looking for the right words. "Do you know what it's like," he asked slowly, "to believe strongly in something, an ideal, a way of life—maybe in spite of evidence to the contrary—and then one day, something happens that makes you question whether or not the belief was ever justified?"

Jain frowned thoughtfully. "Honestly, I'm not sure what you mean. Are we talking about a personal belief, or some external doctrine, created by someone else?"

"Both," he said, relaxing further. It was feeling more like a philosophical discussion than anything else. "What I've been contemplating is how it's possible to hold on to your faith in something—to feel confidence in your ability to upkeep an ideal—when all around you are examples of others who have not. Those who've failed, or changed, good men who've somehow lost sight of that same belief system."

It was as much as he could tell her, and as much as was needed to express the nature of his discontent. He was surprised at how much better he felt already, just speaking his concerns aloud . . . and he realized quite suddenly that he didn't need an answer from her, or from anyone else. Talking about it, acknowledging it, was enough.

And maybe that's what makes the difference, between continuing to fight the good fight and losing one's resolution, one's faith—not to take it for granted. Remembering that it's a choice, every day, just like anything else.

"Do you want to know what I think?" Jain asked, quite seriously. At his nod, she folded her hands in front of her, her tone taking on an edge that he hadn't heard before.

"I think there always has been and always will be people who will uphold their ideals, no matter what—just as there are people who are weak, who will fold when the pressure gets to be too much," she said, looking into his eyes as she spoke. "But I also think that there are those who eventually come to believe that it's not as simple as all that, that there are complexities to be considered beyond black and white, right and wrong. People who start to see that purity of purpose is an illusion. A cloak, really . . . a moralistic disguise, that can actually end up jeopardizing the very ideals they seek to uphold."

She smiled faintly, but not with any reason that he could tell. "It can create quite a paradox, if you think about it—is it wrong to compromise your beliefs in order to preserve them?"

That the question was rhetorical was a relief; Kirk didn't know how to respond, didn't know if she was talking about herself, or openly philosophizing, or expressing serious convictions about morality . . . but he was sure that they'd wandered on to separate tracks. If one had to compromise his own beliefs in order to preserve them, then the beliefs were flawed somehow . . . or the person was.

Jain grinned suddenly, shaking her head. "Listen to me. I'm sorry, I guess that wasn't particularly helpful."

Her smile turned apologetic. "That call a moment ago was something of a summons, I'm afraid. The man I've been working with has an important panel in an hour or so, and I promised to help him prepare."

"I'll walk back with you," Kirk said, disappointed but doing his best to mask it. They'd had such a fine day together, he didn't want it to be over with.

Jain seemed to feel the same way. "If you've got some free time later, maybe we can have dinner . . . or something?"

Being asked out by a beautiful woman was something he could definitely get used to. "I think that can be arranged," he said, smiling.

Together, they left the lounge, Kirk already looking forward to later . . . but he couldn't entirely forget her strange question, or the faint, cheerless smile she'd worn as she asked it—and he realized that he wanted to know who she was more than ever, where she came from, what she did. He'd have to charm her into a few solid answers over dinner . . . or something, as the case might be.

In all, a most engaging day.

Spock reflected over the fascinating itinerary of the summit's second day as he and the captain took seats in the back of the large assembly room, people filing in all around them for the highly anticipated future technologies panel. First, upon arriving, the discussion of energy probabilities in subspace and approaches to discovery. Spock had read several studies on the implementation of strata pulse-testing, but had by no means been convinced that the results would be scientifically sound. From the solid, logical approach of the key speaker to the subject, however, and the well thought out responses from his copanelists, Spock was strongly considering a change of opinion. By opting to leave early in the discussion, the captain had missed a thoroughly captivating aggregation of viewpoints.

Afterward, Spock had briefly vacillated between attending an open debate over harnessing soliton waves or a lecture on perpetuality by Dellas of Tiburon. Soliton wave potential was a particular interest of his, but Dellas was renowned for her powerful and innovative discourses, and seldom appeared before an audience. He had therefore chosen to hear Dellas, and had not been disappointed.

From the lecture, he had planned to attend the dilithium-enhancement discussion, but had ended up in a lengthy conversation with Seren of Vulcan in the corridor outside. Spock had taken note of his own high visibility within the conference, the nods and glances from many of the attendants—the three most likely reasons being his heritage, his past receipt of a Vulcanian science award, and his singular position in Starfleet. It was for the latter that Seren had approached him, to say that his own younger sibling was considering a career in Starfleet, and to ask about Spock's experiences. The conversation had evolved through several fascinating topics thereafter, including non-Federation technology and a panel that Spock had missed by the *Enterprise*'s late arrival, but which Seren had attended, regarding X-ray singularities. There was some slim evidence that the Romulans were turning their attention to the potentially powerful energy source, which lent the possibility more credibility than it had earlier commanded.

The conversation had ended as the dilithium discussion let out, and a most excited Mr. Scott had insisted that they lunch together. Spock had enjoyed their meeting; the engineer lacked the focus of logic, but had been extremely detailed with his own thoughts and projections about the panel he'd attended, enthusiastically expressing his wide knowledge of starship propulsion systems and a number of related subjects.

The afternoon was filled by another lecture, this one on the possibilities of holographic technology; a round-table discussion about the role of science in sociological advancements; and an open discussion on progressions in tachyon communication theory, about which Spock was invited to speak. The captain had attended the last half of the discussion, expressing great pleasure with Spock's contribution when they met afterward.

"Mr. Spock, you almost make me understand it," he'd said, smiling. A great compliment, indeed.

They'd walked together to the future technology panel, the captain choosing seats in the back of the room; as the room filled, his actions suggested that he was searching the crowd for a particular person, his head turning repeatedly, his attention directed and constantly moving.

"Captain, are you expecting to meet someone here?" Spock asked. "If so, perhaps I can help you locate the individual in question. There are eight hundred seats here, and an expectation that all will be filled—"

"Thank you, Mr. Spock, that won't be necessary. She's . . . she's pretty hard to miss," he replied, still scanning the assembling group.

Ah. Perhaps the captain's earlier absence was due to an involvement with a female companion. Spock would not presume to say, although based on past observations, such an assumption would not be illogical.

"There she is."

The captain stood and stepped out into the aisle, his focus on a humanoid woman who had just entered the room. From her flamboyant clothing, Spock had to agree with the captain's earlier assessment.

The woman joined them as the audience began to settle, the first of the panelists moving up onto the raised platform at the front of the room. Spock stood to greet her.

"Dr. Jain Suni, this is my first officer, Mr. Spock."

"A pleasure, Doctor," Spock said politely.

"The pleasure is mine," Dr. Suni replied, nodding in turn. "I read your secondary thesis on charm quark anomalies. Great material."

Before he could respond, the captain pointed out that the panel was about to begin, and the three of them took their seats.

There were six Starfleet scientists on the panel, all well established within their respective fields. Spock had read all of them, although two had stopped publishing in recent years—Dr. Lansing, a researcher in biomechanics, and Dr. Kettaract, a molecular physicist. Of the other four, two were mathematicians, one a geneticist, one a chemical engineer. Dr. Lansing had been chosen as moderator.

Each panelist was introduced, Lansing giving a brief synopsis of each doctor's body of work before opening a general conversation, asking what technological advancements within the Federation could be foreseen for the immediate future and speculation for a century beyond.

As Spock had expected, Dr. Woodmansey spoke first, a geneticist known for his egotism and verbosity. He projected several medical breakthroughs concerning neurological function in the next two decades, theorizing that telekinetic energies might one day provide an inexhaustible source of power. The chemical engineer, Dr. Walse, asked several informed questions, moving the discussion toward exciting new developments in fusion theory. One of the mathematicians brought up Julia set fractal geometry, and Dr. Lansing steered the conversation toward amplification of cellular decay kinetics. It was proving to be an intense and enlightening discussion, the audience quiet, entranced . . . until Dr. Kettaract began to speak.

The molecular physicist, a tall, thin, human male in his late middle age, had remained silent throughout the gentle debate, a brooding look on his face. Spock seemed to recall that Kettaract had been involved in some minor scientific controversy at the beginning of his career, and it appeared that he was determined to continue on his illustrious path.

"All this talk is fine and good," Kettaract began, his thin tone implying otherwise, "but I think we need to talk about *now*—not what the Federation is capable of, or what we're working on, but what the *Klingons* are working on. What the *Romulans* are working on. Because as sure as we sit here, talking about possibilities, talking about incremental steps into the future, they are out there making it happen. And they're making it happen so that they can destroy us, make no mistake. Anyone who doesn't see that is a fool."

A shocked murmur ran through the assembly, the other panelists wearing expressions of irritation, dismay, surprise. Kettaract's aggressive behavior was highly improper for the setting, both disrespectful and inflammatory.

Dr. Lansing made an attempt to refocus attention to the topic. "I'm sure we all understand that the Federation has its enemies, but this is not a political forum. I believe that summit is being held elsewhere."

Laughter fluttered through the audience, but a note of tension ran through it. Lansing continued, making a solid effort to placate the disruptive doctor.

"Dr. Kettaract, perhaps you'd like to share your thoughts on advancements in your own field."

"I apologize if I've been rude," Kettaract said, shaking his head. "But I feel quite strongly that we must address the nature of the environment in which we exist. The Federation is a primarily peaceful community, dedicated to learning, to advancements in science and culture—but we don't operate in a vacuum. And while we're looking for ways to progress, our enemies are looking for a strategic edge. Look at the Romulans—they've been spending their time making improvements to their cloaking technology. And they already have a trade alliance with the Klingons; how long do you think it will be before the first cloaked battle cruiser strikes?"

"What would you propose, *Doctor?*" Woodmansey sneered.

Lansing was on her feet. "Gentlemen, *please*—"

"I propose that we stop wasting our time on the inconsequential, on what *might* be, and start working toward insuring that the Federation will still be here in the future," Kettaract said loudly, his voice rising. "I propose that the Federation's scientific community starts taking a longer view, that we start worrying about how to maintain our superiority as a galactic power!"

People in the audience were standing, arguing, some of them shouting for Kettaract to be removed, others applauding. Dr. Walse left the platform as Lansing stood helplessly, her attempts to bring order frustrated. Not that it mattered; the majority of the assembled scientists had stopped watching the panel, either leaving the room or openly debating among themselves.

"Fascinating," Spock said. He remained in his seat, watching Dr. Kettaract continue his militant rant to members of the audience who had gathered at the base of the platform, offering their own opinions. Spock decided to approach Kettaract when the atmosphere calmed, curious about the evolution of his views.

The captain was also watching the debacle, his eyes narrowed in obvious disapproval—but next to him, Dr. Suni had the fingertips of both hands pressed to the sides of her head, a look of disbelief in her wide eyes. She immediately confirmed her feelings aloud.

"I don't believe it. How could he?"

"You know him?" The captain asked, nodding toward Kettaract.

The doctor sighed heavily. "Bendes Kettaract? Yes, I know him. We came here together; he's the Starfleet scientist I've been working with."

Chapter Eight

Engineering technician Joanna Celaux had been promising Chekov a chess match for a few weeks, but their schedules had not permitted it. Just as he got off a shift, she was going on, and vice versa. Very complicated . . . and also, she had been dating a noncom science technician, some stony-faced dullard named Alec or Alex, he couldn't remember exactly. A decent man, but terribly uninteresting . . . and Chekov knew for a fact that their relationship was not serious, he'd had it from a good source. If he could just arrange one chess game, just one, he was certain that he could impress Joanna into another . . . and then, who knew?

These were the things that Chekov was thinking as he wandered the lower decks, looking for the lovely Miss Celaux. Well, that and a good excuse for his presence in the engineering sections of the ship. He wouldn't want her to think that he had nothing better to do, although in truth, he didn't. With the *Enterprise* sitting perfectly still outside the space station, a number of systems had been transferred over to the computer; only one person was needed to watch the helm, and he had traded shifts with Sulu so that he might catch Joanna before she went off of hers.

He was mentally trying out something casual— Joanna, hello, I was just in the neighborhood to check a relay—when he walked past an open computer maintenance room and heard someone muttering angrily from inside. Chekov could only make out the words *damn* and *blast,* but it was enough. He stopped, curious as to what Dr. McCoy was doing in engineering.

The doctor was sitting with his back to the door, hunched over a computer monitor, still cursing quietly to himself as Chekov walked into the room.

"Dr. McCoy?"

The doctor started, then turned around with a look of perfect irritation. "What is it, Ensign? Can't you see I'm busy?"

Chekov backed up a step, raising his hands. "My apologies, Doctor. I was walking by, and heard you—saying something, that's all. Excuse me."

He turned to leave, but McCoy apparently hadn't finished with him yet. "Why are you skulking around down here, anyway? Don't you have anything better to do?"

Chekov turned back, shrugging. "I was just checking a relay. Sir."

McCoy stared at him, a thoughtful look coming over his scowling face. Chekov waited, wondering if Joanna's shift was over already. He hoped not.

"Mr. Chekov . . ." the doctor said finally, "didn't you tell me the other day that you could find people? With a computer?"

Chekov raised his head proudly. "Yes, sir. If they exist anywhere, I can find them. It's in my blood, you know."

"So I've heard," McCoy said. "I've been trying to track down an old friend of mine . . . a lady friend . . . and I'm not getting anywhere. This is totally unofficial, of course, I'm hoping to avoid any paperwork, or any talk about it—"

Another man searching for love. "Say no more, Doctor. In the words of the great Russian politician Busdeyanov, 'I'm the man for the job.' "

McCoy nodded. "I always wondered who started that. So, how long do you think something like this might take?"

"How long has your friend been missing?"

"Two years."

"She's in Starfleet?"

"No . . . but she's a doctor, a research scientist."

Chekov thought about it, then nodded firmly. "Two days. Three, at most."

McCoy scowled anew. "That long? What are you going to do, send out postcards?"

Awfully touchy for someone asking a favor— though Chekov supposed he could understand. Love made men crazy.

And if Dr. McCoy hasn't seen his lady friend for two years, it's no wonder.

"As I said before, I have a few connections—but it may take some time for them to get back to me, that's all," Chekov said. He actually only had one connection, the younger brother of a friend's friend who happened to work in a Federation records office, and it had been at least a year since they'd last spoken, but Chekov saw no reason that the doctor should know that; chances were good that he'd be able to find McCoy's friend by himself, anyway, and within and hour or two. Most Russians were just naturally computer-savvy, and he was no exception.

"Oh. I see," McCoy said uncertainly. He stood and pulled a data chip out of the console he'd been sitting at, walking over to hand it to him. "Well, here's all the information I have. You won't tell anyone about this . . ."

Chekov was wounded. "Of course not, sir. A man's private affairs are his own business . . . particularly when there's a lady involved."

McCoy coughed, looking away. "Yes, well. You'll come to me as soon as you have anything?"

"You can count on it, Doctor."

The older man stood for another moment, slightly red in the face. When he spoke, it was nearly a mumble. "I, ah, appreciate this, Mr. Chekov."

"Don't even mention it, sir. I know you'd do the same for me." He didn't, actually, but it seemed like the comradely thing to say.

McCoy coughed again, nodded, and quickly left the room.

Proud to be of service, Chekov pocketed the chip—and realized that he now had the perfect excuse to be in engineering. He could tell Joanna that he was helping a friend . . . no, that he was *instrumental* in an investigation to help a friend . . . an officer friend . . . in a matter of utmost importance. A priority matter, about which he'd been sworn to secrecy. Alec or Alex the boring lab technician couldn't possibly compete.

Chekov grinned, images of Joanna's admiring gaze clear in his mind. He patted the chip and went to find her, new hope blooming in his heart like a delicate Russian rose.

As the last of the audience filed out of the conference room, Suni decided that Bendes could go it without her for a little while. How many times had she told him not to get carried away, that there was a time and place for everything? Had he listened? Obviously not. He'd embarrassed himself and her, selfishly spouting off without a thought in his head but how right he was. He was a brilliant scientist, true enough, but the rest of him could stand a major overhaul.

Suni turned to Jim. "I don't want to see him right now. Let's get out of here, I need a drink."

The captain nodded, standing as she did, his first officer doing the same. "I don't blame you. Mr. Spock, would you care to join us?"

Suni could hear a note of reluctance in Jim's invitation, and either Spock heard it, too, or he had other plans. "No, Captain, but thank you. Dr. Suni . . ."

The half Vulcan nodded politely at her. She shot him a brief smile, then turned and walked quickly toward the exit, wanting out before Bendes spotted her among the rapidly waning crowd. After a few words with his first officer, Jim hurried to catch up to her.

The corridor was filled with excited conversation,

the tone of it what one would have expected—disdain for Kettaract and questions about his past, mostly, but also a number of debates about the merits of his statements. A good number of the scientists were Starfleet, and not everyone disagreed with what he'd said.

God, what a mess.

She stared out at the bickering crowd, astounded by Bendes's recklessness.

Jim touched her arm. "Jain, are you all right?"

She nodded, turning to face him. The expression he wore—concern, compassion, his genuine like for her as clear in his eyes as polished dilithium—was touching, if misplaced. She wasn't upset, she was mad as hell. She needed a distraction, she needed to not think about Bendes Kettaract and his destructively self-righteous ego for a little while . . . and she saw the answer in Jim Kirk's sweet expression.

"I'm fine, thank you," she said. "Really, I don't want to talk about it . . . or hear about it, for that matter, and it's going to be all over the station in about ten minutes. There's a bottle of wine in my quarters . . . would you join me?"

She looked into his eyes as she asked it, and saw that he understood the implications of her question. Still, he hesitated a few seconds before answering, and in that small space of time, she saw a depth of deliberate caution and self-control in him that she hadn't suspected. That, and something unfamiliar, something she wasn't sure about until he asked a question of his own.

"Are you sure that's what you want?"

He was trying to watch out for her; he was trying

not to take advantage. That unfamiliar thing was protectiveness, and it made her feel vulnerable to him suddenly, so much so that she almost retracted her invitation . . . but at the same time, his chivalrous warmth thrilled her, it made her want him even more. To be alone with him, to be touched by him, looking into his eyes and seeing what she saw now . . .

"I'm sure," she said, her heart beating faster at the gentle smile her response elicited. "Positive."

He offered her his arm and the two of them started down the corridor, the thought of Bendes Kettaract seeming like the least important thing in the universe, second only to the irony of her sudden intense desire for James Kirk.

Spock waited until the small, enthusiastic crowd surrounding Dr. Kettaract gradually melted away before approaching, hoping to receive the doctor's undivided attention. He was still unable to recall the reason by which he associated Kettaract's past with conflict, but had already decided that he would investigate the matter upon returning to the *Enterprise*.

Kettaract was following his last supporter toward the doors of the conference room when Spock stepped up to meet him.

"Dr. Kettaract. I'm wondering if I might have a moment of your time."

Kettaract turned to look at him, his reaction upon seeing Spock one of surprised recognition . . . turning quickly to a guarded wariness. The doctor folded his arms, staring steadily at him.

"You're Spock. From the *Enterprise*."

"I am."

"Tell me," Kettaract asked, a note of challenge in his voice, "have I merited your support or your condemnation?"

"Neither, sir," Spock said. "I'm merely curious. The fervency with which you have expressed yourself is uncommonly strong."

Kettaract laughed suddenly, a high, harsh sound that indicated scorn or derision—though Spock did not believe it was directed at him. "And you want to know why, is that right? You, of all people."

Spock was puzzled by his reaction. "I fail to see, sir, why my interest might be distinct from another's."

"Do you really?"

The physicist glanced around the nearly empty room before leaning forward, his voice lowered as if in confidence. "After what you did to even out the playing field, as it were, you and your good friend Captain Kirk—you expect me to believe that you don't understand where I'm coming from?"

Not willing to deny some understanding, Spock didn't answer, waiting for him to expand, to clarify—although Kettaract's open accusation could only be about the theft of the Romulan cloaking device. Considering the covert nature of the mission, Spock was quite surprised that Kettaract was aware of it—and even more so that he appeared willing, even eager to volunteer his knowledge.

"Starfleet Intelligence called me in to study it," Kettaract said, his tone flat with anger. "Whenever they get their hands on some piece of advanced alien technology, I'm one of the first ones they call. In fact, Starfleet is currently preparing sensor-array upgrades based on my report."

"And because of this, you feel that I possess a particular awareness of your feelings regarding Federation technology?" Spock asked, choosing his words carefully. He did not share Kettaract's rather casual attitude toward disclosure—and as fascinated as he was by the unusual conversation, he was forced by personal conviction and duty to consider its cessation.

At his question, Kettaract's demeanor changed, turning from anger to what Spock perceived as frustration.

"We have the technology," Kettaract said. "Starfleet has the means to make a decisive stand against its enemies, and it's just *sitting* there, collecting dust. And all because the Federation wants to play fair, they want to pretend that they're too good to resort to anything so unflattering as winning. It's a pretense of virtue, a sham."

Spock nodded, understanding finally. "You object to Starfleet's policy against the use of certain technologies that they have acquired."

"Obviously," Kettaract snapped—and then frowned, peering closely at Spock. "And actually, I don't understand why you don't. You're a Vulcan. They ordered you to lie and steal, I read the report . . . tell me, how did you rationalize it, Mr. Spock? And how do you now rationalize the hypocrisy that your mission and its outcome has exposed?"

The questions were valid, but unacceptable. Spock had not admitted to anything, nor could he. "I am unable to respond, sir."

Kettaract nodded. "Of course not. But if I were you, I would consider it, because you never know when things might change. The Federation wants to set an example, they want everything to evolve at a nice, even pace, so that nobody can win. But if Starfleet ever gets hold of something *truly* significant, do you honestly doubt they'll hesitate in using it?"

Spock was considering a response in spite of the question's rhetorical nature, when Kettaract's communicator sounded. The doctor pulled it from his belt and flipped it open, half turning away from Spock.

"Kettaract."

"Dr. Kettaract, this is M-20 Communications." A young male voice. Spock could hear him clearly. "Sir, we've just received a text message field for you . . ."

"Go ahead."

"Actually, sir, there *is* no message," the young male said. "Only the name of the sender was received, one, ah, John Hermes, but the field was blank."

Kettaract glanced at Spock. "John Hermes . . . no message? Can you trace the line back?"

"No, sir, I'm sorry. It came in through the main sector relay."

"Figures," Kettaract said, sighing. "Thank you."

He closed the communicator, facing Spock again. "Technology at its finest. Well. As much as I've enjoyed our little nonconversation, I imagine my welcome at this conference is about to be rescinded, and I'd like to leave before I'm forced to. If you'll excuse me, Commander."

Spock nodded, although he doubted very much that the summit organizers would eject the physicist. Kettaract walked away, his thin shoulders hunched, already reaching for his communicator again.

He stood for a moment, considering Bendes Kettaract . . . and decided that he would return to the *Enterprise* promptly, his curiosities only heightened by their brief encounter. Spock decided also that his earlier assessment of the day as "engaging" had been accurate, but much too mild a sentiment.

Jain's rooms were much like Darres's, plush but nondescript, and by unspoken agreement, they left the lights low. They chatted about nothing at all—a childhood pet, a memory from school—as she uncorked the wine, a kind of burgundy, Jain sticking to her resolution not to discuss Kettaract or the panel. She poured each of them a full glass before joining Kirk on the couch, and drank half of hers in one swallow before leaning back against the cushions, sighing heavily.

"Excuse me," she said, smiling. "I believe it's supposed to be sipped."

"I believe you're right," Kirk said, tasting from his glass. The wine was rich and sweet, very good. He was about to say as much when Jain took another deep swallow and set her glass aside, moving closer. Her leg touched his, and he felt a surge of warmth, of want, as she reached out and plucked the wineglass from his willing fingers. She put it on the low table in front of the couch before turning to face him, moving still closer—and although her intent was obvious, he saw a trace of uncertainty in her eyes, the same he'd seen outside the conference room.

As she leaned forward, he reached out and cupped her face with both hands, stopping her.

"Jain . . ." He searched her face, searched for words that would express all the things he wanted to tell her—that she was beautiful, smart, exciting, that he wanted to kiss her, to make love to her, but . . .

"We don't have to hurry," he said, meaning it for her sake. "It's all right with me if we don't—if you—"

"Kiss me," she whispered, and the last of his reserve fell away. He pulled her close, kissing her, marveling at the softness of her lips and skin, at the sweet taste of burgundy and her mouth, at the scent of her hair, like peaches. Her arms came up across his back, a soft, yearning sound in her throat as her fingers twined through his hair—

—and her communicator beeped. Once. Again. A third time.

Against him, Jain had tensed. Kirk reluctantly broke their kiss, unable to help a smile at the look of black irritation on her face as she leaned away from him, fumbling at her belt.

"Somebody hates me," she said, standing. She opened the device, running a hand through her hair.

"Suni."

"Jain, it's Bendes. I'm—"

"Hang on," she said, glancing apologetically at Kirk before walking toward the bedroom.

Kirk took a deep breath and blew it out, reaching for his glass. He could hear the angry tone of her voice if not her words, and from the sound of it, he almost felt sorry for Kettaract.

Almost. The smell of peaches still lingered.

He clearly heard her ask, "John? Not Tom, you're sure?," and then her voice lowered, became serious, barely audible.

Kirk sipped his wine, impatient for her return. Any suspicion of uncertainty on her part was gone, lost in the total abandonment with which she'd returned his kiss . . .

"Jim."

He looked up, saw her standing in the bedroom's entrance—and knew immediately, from the look on her face and the unhappiness with which she'd spoken his name, that something had come up.

Kirk put down his glass and stood, straightening his uniform, wishing that communicators didn't exist. Jain moved to stand in front of him, the disappointment clear on her face.

"I'm so sorry," she said, taking his hand. "Bendes—Dr. Kettaract—has decided that it's time for us to leave. He's already at the ship, and I've got about five minutes to get there. Believe me, if there was any way . . ."

Kirk forced a smile. "Where are you going?"

"Back to the lab—Jim, the project we've been working on, it's going to be over with soon. My part in it, anyway—"

"How soon?" He asked, gazing down into her astounding eyes. Scientific consultants had traveled on the *Enterprise* before, many times.

"Maybe a few weeks. Maybe only days," she said.

"How can I contact you?" he asked, brushing her dark hair away from her forehead.

"You can't, and please don't try," she said. "It's a

security matter, I'm sorry. But I can get in touch with you . . . if you want."

"I want." He leaned over and kissed her firmly, already wistful for her as she walked him to the door. He offered to see her to her ship but she shook her head, sounding just as wistful as he felt.

"It's better this way," she said, stopping just short of triggering the door. "More private."

They embraced, tightly, and said good-bye, and then he was alone, the door closed between them.

Chapter Nine

Returning to the *Enterprise* almost a full hour before the captain, Spock had ample time to research Bendes Kettaract—and to look into circumstances which might prove valuable in the imminent future, depending on his conversation with Kirk. Spock had asked to be alerted when the captain called for transport, arriving just as he was walking out of the transporter room.

"Mr. Spock, I thought you'd still be at the conference," the captain said. He appeared to be tired, his shoulders somewhat slumped as he started toward his quarters. Spock fell in beside him.

"After speaking with Dr. Kettaract, I decided that my time would be better spent here, researching his personal and professional history," Spock responded. "And I've uncovered a few facts that bear immediate discussion."

"Explain."

Spock quickly related the gist of his conversation with Kettaract, which surprised and concerned the captain. They reached his quarters as Spock was relating the information, the captain gesturing him inside so that he could continue.

"His willingness to discuss the cloaking device, and his excessive anger toward what he considers to be Starfleet's hypocrisy, prove nothing," Spock said.

The captain leaned against the edge of his desk, crossing his arms. "But?"

"There is a history of emotional instability. Bendes Kettaract achieved his first doctorate at the age of nineteen, in molecular physics, and went on to earn two more before he was twenty-five, in quantum mechanics and chemistry. He was enrolled in Starfleet Academy throughout, and was regarded as something of a prodigy even before his first paper was published, on proton decay. Afterward, the Federation's scientific community unofficially designated his as the next great mind in science. Kettaract then disappeared for two years, throwing himself into a new project—and upon his next publication, he became an object of scorn to the same people who had earlier embraced him. He theorized a stable, energy-producing, artificially created molecule that would 'be to a warp core what a warp core is to a matchstick,' and was denounced as a fool when serious flaws in his premise became immediately apparent."

The captain raised one hand slightly, stopping him. "Is it possible, his theory?"

"No," Spock answered. "However, having read his paper, I believe he was much closer than anyone credited. His math was superb, and all of the components he based his theory around do exist. If such a synthesis was possible, the energy output would be as high as he postulated, perhaps higher. But the design was inherently unstable, and that instability meant his molecule could not exist for more than a fraction of a second."

Although Spock could have continued, the captain nodded, and he returned to Kettaract's history.

"The barrage of denouncements from his peers drove him out of the public eye for just over a decade," Spock continued. "It is unknown what he did for the entire period, but he was hospitalized twice for paranoid episodes in the first five years, claiming that he was being watched and followed. He apparently recovered; at the end of his hiatus, he published again—this time, a speculative analysis of a theoretical quark grouping. The paper was heralded as brilliant, and did much to redeem his reputation, although not to the same status as before.

"Since then, Kettaract has worked in and out of the private sector, primarily as a researcher but also as a consultant, among other things. Technically, he is still a member of Starfleet, but has not been considered to be on active duty for some time. As he told me himself, he's done work for Starfleet Intelligence . . . and it was his reference to the Romulan cloaking device that drew my attention—"

"—because of the *Sphinx*," the captain said softly. "Have you found any evidence of a connection between Kettaract and Casdcn?"

"I have not," Spock said. "I have nothing but conjecture at this point."

"But you think you're on to something, don't you?"

Spock raised an eyebrow. "I believe further investigation is not unwarranted, sir."

The captain paused, frowning. His voice when he spoke was uncertain. "Is it possible . . . do you believe that Dr. Suni might know something about this?"

"I would not presume to say," Spock said. "Logically, however, it must be considered. By Dr. Suni's own admission, the two of them are currently working together on an unspecified project—of which there is no mention in the files."

The captain nodded reluctantly, clearly dissatisfied with the conclusion. "Yes, of course. Recommendations?"

"First, that we coordinate with Captain Darres's investigation," Spock said. "His team may have access to information about Jack Casden and the *Sphinx* that we do not. I also recommend a more exhaustive search of Federation records for information about Doctors Kettaract and Suni, perhaps cross-referencing with M-20's files. And I suggest that we concern ourselves with whether or not Captain Casden was actually involved with the Romulans—which, based on my conversation with Dr. Kettaract, we can no longer presume with any certainty. We have to account for the *Sphinx*'s graviton reading, and if the device we obtained is still being studied by Starfleet Intelligence—"

The captain finished his thought. "—then where did that reading come from?" He looked at Spock closely, pursing his lips. "How do you propose we do that, exactly?"

"By speaking with the Romulan Commander," Spock said. "She is still in Federation space."

"Still?" the captain asked. "But why? The Federation doesn't hold political prisoners . . . surely there wasn't a problem with physically returning her."

"She's to be exchanged for a Federation ambassadorial aide being held by the Romulans, on charges of espionage," Spock said. "The commander is not a prisoner. She's being detained on Starbase 23, near the Neutral Zone, but has been allowed free access to contact her people, within security-based limits. This personnel exchange was insisted upon by the Romulan government, apparently so that their release of the ambassadorial aide will not be taken as a sign of weakness, by their enemies or their own populace."

The next logical step was obvious. Starbase 23 was barely eight light-years from Station M-20.

"Sir, I request permission to leave at once for Starbase 23 and speak with the Romulan commander."

The captain raised his eyebrows. "You think she'll talk to you?"

Spock hesitated, considering what he knew of her. "I believe it's quite possible."

The captain nodded once. "Permission granted. I'll ask Captain Darres to lend us one of his ships, first thing in the morning. M-20 has two personal transports with warp capability; you can be there and back in hours instead of days."

Spock agreed, and after a few possibilities were discussed concerning the expansion of the file searches, Spock was dismissed. He headed for the bridge to see about establishing a temporary computer link between the file libraries of the *Enterprise* and M-20, and realized upon his arrival that for several minutes, he had focused his thoughts on the relatively simple task to the exclusion of all else. He had been avoiding thoughts of the commander, and the recognition of his internal evasion gave him pause. Retreat from oneself indicated an emotional reaction.

Spock contacted the starbase and secured a connection between their records libraries, asking the ship's computer to compile data on Bendes Kettaract, Jain Suni, and Jack Casden. After a brief consideration, he added the name John Hermes, the sender of Dr. Kettaract's unwritten message.

He expected the complete search to take several hours, and decided that he would retire to his quarters, to consider his upcoming conversation with the commander, assuming that she would agree to see him.

His unusual effort to avoid thinking of her also required contemplation; he was the first officer of the ship, and ship's business demanded that someone contact an emissary of the Romulan government in order to collect information. Considering that the commander was available, and that the two of them had briefly established a personal connection, it was only logical that he should make the attempt.

Spock kept that firmly in mind as he walked to his quarters. It was all a matter of logic.

Kirk woke up early and contacted Darres about letting Spock use a personal transport. Darres agreed, and Kirk invited him to the *Enterprise* for lunch, telling him that he wanted to talk more extensively about Jack Casden. He didn't explain why; considering Darres's feelings about Casden, Kirk thought a face-to-face would be better.

He and Spock went over the results of the computer search, which had turned up very little; there was nothing on Jain but an educational history, and nothing further on Kettaract or Casden. When Spock explained the reference to John Hermes—there was no file for anyone by that name currently living in Federation space—Kirk remembered that Jain had said something like "Tom, not John" to Kettaract the night before. Spock ran the name Tom Hermes, but again, they came up empty.

Spock beamed over to the station, and had departed for Starbase 23 by 0900. Kirk saw him off the ship, and though he thought his friend's trip was a good idea—logical—he had to wonder if the Romulan commander would agree to see him. Obviously, Spock wouldn't deign to discuss it, but Kirk wasn't blind; the commander had been interested in Spock personally, and they *had* spent a good period of time alone together . . . although the thought of Mr. Spock being anything less than purely professional with a Federation enemy, even an attractive one, was pretty hard to swallow. Still, *Hell hath no fury,* as the saying went, and unless he'd misread the commander's signals toward his first officer, he thought Spock might end up getting the door slammed in his face.

With only a minimum of ship's affairs to see to, Kirk found himself looking for ways to kill time before meeting with Darres. Bones was still busy with the crew physicals, obviously caught up in one of his workaholic phases, and although about fifty crew members were attending the third day of the summit, give or take, Kirk decided that he didn't feel like returning to M-20; he went to the ship's gym instead and spent an hour at the punching bag and weights, his thoughts full of Jain.

All they knew for certain about Kettaract was that he was angry, political, and that he knew about the cloaking device—but if it turned out to be more than that, if they discovered that Kettaract's knowledge of the cloak was somehow connected to what happened to the *Sphinx,* then there was a possibility that Jain might know something. After their incredible day together, he couldn't believe that she would involve herself in anything immoral or unethical—she was too bright, too straightforward—but he kept returning to the conversation they'd had, in the observation lounge. What she'd said, about compromising one's beliefs in order to hold on to them . . . maybe she'd found out something about Kettaract, something she felt she couldn't reveal. It would explain her strange statement—and it would mean that she hadn't actually participated in anything untoward, which was what he wanted more than anything to believe.

It was hard not to wonder. Jain was something of a paradox unto herself, honest with her opinions and feelings, cryptic and vague when it came to actual information about her life or work. And that all the computer had on her was a list of schools she'd attended was certainly unusual, especially considering her claim to be working on a Starfleet project.

The captain showered and dressed, and was just leaving the gym when Uhura called, her voice spilling out of the intercom by the door.

"Bridge to Captain Kirk."

He stepped to the wall, tapping the switch. "Kirk here."

"Sir, I have Captain Gage Darres from M-20 on the line; he says it's important."

"Put him through," Kirk said, frowning. It was already 1100, they'd be meeting in an hour, and Darres wasn't the type to get overly excited about trivial matters—

"Go ahead, Captain," Uhura said.

"Jim?"

"Yes, I'm here," Kirk said.

Darres sounded slightly out of breath. "I need to come up to the ship, now. Will you meet me in your transporter room?"

"Of course—what is it? Is something wrong?"

"I don't think it's safe to talk about it," Darres said, his breathing ragged. "I coded my notes, but I'm pretty sure now that my temp quarters are bugged. I'm calling from ops, but they could be monitoring everything, this could be huge—"

"Slow down," Kirk said, alarmed at Darres's obvious fear; he'd never seen or heard it before. "Who's 'they'?"

"Will you meet me? Right now?" He sounded on the verge of panic.

"Yes," Kirk said firmly. "Gage, listen to me—call security, have someone escort you to the transporter room. Will you do that?"

Darres took a deep breath, blew it out. "Okay. I'm

okay, I just—right after I talked to you, I got this call, and—"

"You can tell me about it when you get here. I'll see you in a few minutes. Kirk out."

After a brief call to engineering, Kirk walked quickly to the transporter room, deeply concerned. Either Darres was having some kind of burnout, brought on by the stress of the investigation, or his safety really had been compromised somehow. Neither option seemed preferable. He'd talked to Darres only a few hours ago, and he'd been fine; if he was suffering from paranoid delusions at the time, he'd hidden it well . . .

. . . which suggests that there really is a "they."

Scotty was on the transporters, and was locking on the station's signal when Kirk arrived.

"We're all set to receive, Captain."

Kirk nodded, watching the empty platform impatiently. Another minute slowly passed before Mr. Scott announced the incoming signal, much to Kirk's relief.

In front of them, a single, shifting glitter of light and shadow spun up, solidifying, becoming Gage Darres—

—and as the shimmering pattern turned solid, Darres collapsed, crumpling boneless to the platform, his eyes wide and staring.

Kirk was crouching at his side in a second, barely hearing Mr. Scott call for medical assistance as he lifted his old friend, supporting him into a half-sitting position, calling his name.

Gage Darres didn't answer. He was dead.

* * *

Because the fatality was recorded as having occurred on board the *Enterprise,* it fell to McCoy to perform the autopsy. And because it had been one of Jim's friends who'd died, McCoy worked fast. He was ready to deliver his report less than two hours after he'd first been called to the transporter room by Mr. Scott.

After seeing that the remains were securely stored, McCoy washed up and called Jim to sickbay—and realized, with a guilty start, that the autopsy had been a relief, in a way. As tragic as unexpected death was, it had a way of reminding people that they were still alive . . . and sometimes that went for doctors, too. Maybe especially, because a big part of the medical profession was about dealing with death, and about maintaining an objectivity when faced with the pitiful truth of it.

Strange, how that carefully trained objectivity seems to miss a beat, when it's your own lifeless face you imagine staring up at you.

McCoy ignored the thought, reminding himself that he had to think positive. Counting on Chekov to come through with Karen Patterson's whereabouts made it a little harder, but surely the young man's ego would push him to succeed, come hell or high water. Chekov would find Karen, and if there was a treatment available anywhere in the universe, she'd know about it.

While he waited for Jim, McCoy went through Darres's personals, picking out the data chip he'd found tucked into the captain's right boot. He walked to the computer, curious about what might be on the chip, primarily because it was a strange place to carry one. Since the only DNA trace on the thing came from the dead man, there was no physical evidence to preserve, and therefore no reason not to look.

McCoy plugged it in—and a series of symbols came up on the screen, a seemingly endless stream of them interspersed with a few numbers. He asked the computer to translate, but it turned out not to be a language, or at least not one on file. Sighing, McCoy pulled the chip just as Jim walked in, his face set in the grim lines of a man dealing with an unforeseen grief. McCoy suddenly felt selfish, for worrying about his own problems when Jim's friend had died.

The captain didn't waste time on pleasantries. "Well?"

"Well, as far is I can tell, it was an accident," McCoy said, standing up. "Transporter failure—theirs, not ours—and the most common kind there is, cellular shock. Things don't fit back together quite right. It's almost always an internal tissue mismatch, the wrong types of cells being used to rebuild something inside, often the heart; the body can't take it and shuts down."

Jim didn't respond, staring down at the floor, his expression blank.

McCoy softened his tone. "It happened fast, Jim. He wouldn't have suffered."

The captain looked up. "So it was a transporter malfunction. On the station."

"That's right."

"Could it have been done on purpose?"

McCoy blinked, surprised at the question. Jim had

asked him to check for anything unusual, by which he'd assumed tissue damage or toxins in the system, but there hadn't been anything like that. If someone had actually rigged the transporter to fail . . . why, that was cold-blooded murder, plain and simple.

"I don't know," McCoy said. "It seems unlikely that someone would go through that kind of trouble . . ."

"But is it *possible?*" Jim asked.

McCoy scowled. "I'm a doctor, not a technician. Ask Scotty, or Spock."

Jim nodded slowly. "Good idea. I'm not sure when Spock's getting back, but I was planning to send Mr. Scott over to look for bugs, anyway, and see about their investigation. I'll have him check out their systems."

Where did Spock go? Bugs?

"Sounds like I've missed a few things lately," McCoy said slowly.

"You have," Jim said, his voice a bit gruff. "I'll be happy to fill you in when you've got a spare minute. Are you almost done with the physicals?"

McCoy started to bristle at Jim's tone, but gave up after about two seconds. He'd been avoiding his friends for days. Expecting that no one would notice or care was ridiculous.

"I'll probably be finished early tomorrow," McCoy said.

"Good," Jim said, and then in a lighter tone, "because you know how Spock gets when you're not around."

McCoy smiled. "Mouthy?"

Jim smiled back. "Bored."

It was only a second or two before their smiles faded, as though the weight of their troubles was too great to be suspended any longer, but it was time enough for McCoy to understand how lonely he'd been.

Tell him.

No. Not until he'd talked to Karen, not until the outcome was certain.

"Anything else?" Jim asked.

"Actually, there is." McCoy picked up the data chip. "I found this tucked in one of his boots. I opened it up, but it's just a bunch of symbols and numbers. The computer couldn't read it, either."

Kirk took it from him. "Darres said something about putting his notes into code. He thought he was being targeted because of his investigation into what happened on the *Sphinx*."

That explained a few things. No wonder Jim was talking about bugs and computer mistakes-on-purpose.

"Uhura might be able to do something with it," the captain continued, heading toward the door. "Thanks, Bones."

"Don't mention it," McCoy said. "And Jim . . . I'm sorry about your friend."

"Me, too," Jim said.

Chapter Ten

The journey from Deep Space Station M-20 to Starbase 23 was brief and uneventful, and Spock used the time to hypothesize connections between Dr. Kettaract and what had happened to the *Sphinx*. He considered a wide range of motivations and goals, from Kettaract being in collusion with the Romulans to his stealing the cloaking technology in some plot against the Federation. Obviously, without additional information, not one of his theories could claim a solid foundation of fact—however, he found that the running speculation kept his mind occupied . . . and when new data did present itself, there was always the possibility that it would support a premise he had already structured.

Upon his arrival, the transport and his person were scanned by security personnel, a standard practice for the starbase; its proximity to the Neutral Zone demanded heightened safety measures. When careful scrutiny had classified him as a nonthreat, he was issued a pass and asked to wait while the Romulan commander was informed of his arrival. Because she was a guest of the station, she was not required to submit to any interviews.

Spock was kept waiting for nearly an hour before the commander made her decision, which was to grant him some of her time. He had expected to wait, because he believed that she did not wish to seem overly eager, either to dismiss or accept him. She was a proud woman; she was Romulan.

He was led to her somewhat isolated rooms by the station manager's aide and left there after a brief lecture concerning disclosure of Starfleet or Federation business, the lecture's summary being not to do so. He was also informed that while her communications with her own government were monitored for content, her quarters were private.

Standing outside her door, Spock mentally collected himself in preparation for the interview and then signaled his presence.

"Enter," she said, the sound of her voice surprising him somehow, and he stepped inside.

She was sitting at a small table in the middle of the living space, an empty chair across from her; the room's padded couch and chairs had been pushed aside. He noted that the air was pleasantly warm, the environment similar to that of his quarters on the *Enterprise,* and to her own ship.

He turned his attention to the commander, and she returned it evenly, neither of them speaking. As with the sound of her voice, seeing her again was oddly surprising, his body reacting as if to a minor shock—although except for a change in the style of her hair, which was pinned up, she was as he remembered. Elegant, with a presence that demanded attention and respect.

"Hello, Spock," she said, her tone without inflection. She gestured to the chair opposite her own. "Would you care to sit?"

"Yes, thank you," he replied, moving to join her. When he was seated, he and the commander again studied one another, his fascination drawn to her eyes. There were complexities there that he had not forgotten, her gaze as disturbing to him as it had been at their first meeting. Disturbing, but not distressing.

"You didn't say good-bye to me when I left the *Enterprise,*" she said, gently but with no artifice of kindness. Her voice was deep and tuneful. "Have you come to apologize?"

"That is not the purpose of my visit," he said. "But if my actions or lack thereof offended you, I apologize."

She watched him, smiling slightly. "Then I accept. Tell me, what is the reason for your visit? I doubt very much that it's the pleasure of my company."

He felt an urge to disagree with her, in spite of the truth of her statement; he suppressed it. "I've come to ask for information regarding cloaking technology and the distribution of it within the Romulan Empire."

Her smile widened, but he could see clearly that anger inspired it. "You're joking—no, of course you're not. Why? And what makes you think that I'd want to help you?"

Spock had already considered answers to her questions. "The *Enterprise* is currently investigating an event which may have involved a cloaking device. There are rumors being passed that your people were involved with this event, in which a number of deaths occurred—but there's also a possibility that the matter is an internal one. I seek the truth, and would use your answers only for the purposes of defining this investigation. I would not betray your confidence."

"Really?" she asked airily. "How comforting. And what if I told you that the Empire is planning a hostile invasion of Federation space?"

"Obviously, I have to consider the sanctity of life paramount," he said.

"Obviously," she said, watching him intently. "But you still haven't answered my question. You've told me why I should help you ... but you haven't yet explained why you feel that I might wish to."

Spock considered his response carefully. He understood that she was searching for his personal assessment of their relationship, but the truth did not reflect well on his commitment to the Vulcan identity. What made it all the more difficult was that she had made her own feelings clear, all those weeks ago, that she accepted and even encouraged his humanity—at the same time respecting his choice to identify himself as Vulcan. It was an acceptance that he had rarely known, and never from a woman to whom he was attracted.

He had come to ask a favor. He would not lie.

"My hope is that the time we spent together transcended our respective politics," Spock said. "I feel that you might want to assist me now because the brief intimacy between us contained no betrayal of emotion. The actions surrounding our encounter, my actions, did not honor that connection, but in my mind, the closeness remains untouched by treachery."

The sharpness of her demeanor softened, her expression relaxing. "I see."

When she didn't expand on her understanding, Spock decided to repeat his request. "Will you speak to me regarding cloaking technology?"

The commander sighed. "You tempt me . . . but I've known you to lie, Spock, and trusting you now would be idiocy on my part. When I return to Romulan space, I expect to be stripped of my command because of you and your captain. Fortunately, both my bloodline and the Senate's desire to hold my failures up as an example of Federation deceit put some value on my life, or I would be facing execution as well."

It was unfortunate that she would not speak with him. He acknowledged his responsibility for her circumstances and prospects. "I am sorry."

She smiled faintly at him. "Don't be. You'd be dead by my order if your mission had failed, the *Enterprise* destroyed. Things are as they are. And though I would like to believe you . . ."

Her eyes narrowed, the sudden change in her face indicating that she'd thought of something to make her trust possible.

"There is a way. Share your mind with me, Spock. If I can know that you're telling the truth—if we form a link and I see that you can be trusted, that your purpose is not to deceive, I'll speak to you."

Spock saw a tenuous logic to her proposal, although his initial instinct was to reject it. The mindmeld was deeply personal, an intimacy that far surpassed the gentle emotional probings of their last experience . . .

. . . but the information she possesses could be of vital importance—and I have linked before as a matter of furthering a Starfleet agenda . . .

He recognized that he was, in part, seeking a rationalization—because a part of him wanted very much to open up to the commander, to experience her thoughts and feelings as she searched his consciousness for intent. The indulgence was unacceptable, even distasteful; however, refusing the link for personal reasons was even more so. Logically, the reasons for participating outweighed the reasons to resist participation.

"Very well," he said, committing himself—and was unable to deny an anticipatory flush of thought and sensation as the commander stood and walked to the couch, her apparent indifference to his acquiescence somehow responsible for exciting his curiosity further.

After giving the coded data chip to Lieutenant Uhura, Kirk went to his quarters and sat for a while, thinking. His sorrow and anger were in balance for a time, but anger gradually began to take over. Gage Darres was dead, and there was no doubt that it was murder, not to him, not after Darres's call. Scotty had gone to the station to see what he could find, but with as strange and unresolved as things had been lately—Casden, the investigation, Jain and Kettaract—Kirk wasn't betting on his engineer turning up anything solid.

Gage had it right all along ... or someone thought he did, someone who wanted to shut him up. But what had Darres actually known? He'd believed that Casden was diehard loyal to Starfleet, that it was a setup—but if so, why? And there was Spock's unavoidable conclusion, that such an operation absolutely required a conspiracy ... but who, and how many? What objective was supposed to be served by murdering Casden and his crew?

And now Gage, too, like a cover-up of a cover-up. Whatever was going on, it had to be stopped. Too many had died already.

It kept coming back to the Federation's recently acquired cloaking technology ... and that bothered him, for more than one reason. If someone with less than honorable intentions got hold of a cloaking device—which might have already happened—they could do an extraordinary amount of damage, putting lives in jeopardy, even inciting a war among the galaxy's major powers.

On its own, that was bad enough—but added to the mix was the unhappy possibility that he was to blame, at least partially. Rear Admiral Cartwright might have given the order, but he'd carried it out. He couldn't disown his part in bringing the technology to the Federation, and even the idea of it made him feel sick. That graviton reading had come from somewhere, and if the Romulans weren't responsible for what happened to the *Sphinx*, it seemed likely that the technology had been seized from Starfleet Intelligence. Maybe by Kettaract, maybe by somebody else, but it didn't really matter; if he hadn't taken the device, there wouldn't have been anything to seize.

As it usually did when he was feeling sorry for himself, his internal voice spoke up, taking him to task.

You can brood about it or you can act. Do something, do anything, *just don't sit still wishing things were different.*

Kirk stood up from the edge of the bed and walked to his desk, tapping the intercom button as he sat down. "Kirk to bridge."

"Yes, Captain, this is Lieutenant Uhura."

"Any luck with that chip, Lieutenant?" He didn't expect results so soon after giving it to her, but it was worth asking.

"Not yet, sir," she said, sounding faintly discouraged. "It's a complicated code."

"I have faith in you, Lieutenant," he said. "But take a break for a moment, if you don't mind—contact Commodore Jefferson at Starbase 27 for me, and pipe it to my quarters . . . and see if you can locate Admiral Cartwright's current whereabouts, and request an interview. I believe he's at Starbase 29."

"Yes, sir. Stand by, please."

Kirk waited, tapping his fingers on the desktop, not quite sure what he was hoping to find out . . . but the information that Commodore Jefferson had passed along about Casden had to have come from somewhere—and if Darres was right, if the rumors were lies, tracking down the source could be important.

As for Cartwright . . . he'd assigned the *Enter-*

prise to retrieve a cloaking device from a Romulan ship, by any means necessary. The mission had been an unusual one, and though Kirk had carried out his orders faithfully and without question, he'd wondered more than once from whom the admiral had received *his* orders. Cartwright had handed down the assignment without explaining anything, and had struck Kirk as something of a blowhard—

Uhura interrupted his wondering thoughts. "Captain, I've reached Starbase 27, but it appears that Commodore Jefferson has been reassigned. I have a Commander Lewis on line with that information."

Strange. "Put it through."

Lewis was an older woman with dark hair and an artificial smile, who introduced herself as being in charge of personnel placement for Starbases 25 through 30.

Kirk got straight to the point. "Commander, where's Commodore Jefferson?"

Lewis shook her head, her expression quickly turning sour. "I don't know, sir. The whole situation is most irregular—Commodore Jefferson's placement here was apparently temporary, he was here less than three months and his security status did not require him to explain his business to me." Her voice had taken on the defensively pedantic tone of a minor bureaucrat, unhappy with being bypassed. "Two days ago, I received the standard 344-B data excusing him from duty, straight from Starfleet Command. No explanation, no sector designation. He left only a few hours after receiving his leave."

Lewis shook her head again. "Most irregular," she repeated.

Kirk thanked her and broke the connection, not sure what to think. He wasn't one for coincidences, but he couldn't imagine any reasonable alternative—

"Uhura to Captain Kirk. I have Rear Admiral Cartwright standing by, from Starbase 29."

The communications lieutenant sounded taken aback, and Kirk felt much the same. It usually took hours, even days to get a call back from a man like Cartwright, a high-ranking and highly placed administrator still on his way up. It had been less than ten minutes since he'd asked Uhura to find him.

"Put him through."

Cartwright appeared on the screen, stiff and unsmiling. "What is it, Captain? I'm a busy man."

Apparently not *that* busy. "Of course, Admiral. I was hoping to discuss a recent assignment with you, regarding a Starfleet Intelligence matter—"

"This is a secure line," Cartwright said, almost derisively. "You can speak freely."

"Yes, sir," Kirk said politely, though not without some effort. The admiral wasn't going to give him any information if he pushed—and like it or not, the man was a superior officer, and deserved some respect. "It's about the cloaking device. I was curious, sir, about the origins behind that mission. If—"

Cartwright interrupted. "Captain, you did a fine job," he said, his tone flat and uninterested, as if he was reciting memorized lines. "You should feel proud to have contributed so much to the continued security and safety of the Federation. But your orders have been fulfilled, and Starfleet Intelligence has the ball now. Your part in all that is over—and considering the delicate nature of what transpired, it seems to me that you shouldn't be concerning your-self any further."

He smiled then, but the smile didn't reach his eyes. "Is that all?"

So it seems. "Yes, sir."

"Fine. Good day, Captain."

Cartwright faded out, and Kirk stared at the blank screen, thinking that the scope of his concerns just kept growing, his unease deepening, but in a vague, nebulous way that made it nearly impossible to pin down. It seemed like the more information he got, the less things made sense.

He hoped that Spock was having better luck, and that he'd return soon with something that might actually help—because at the moment, Kirk was feeling pretty damned helpless.

She'd thought often of what had happened between them since coming to Starbase 23, the memories of that single day filling her with anger, hurt, disappointment . . . embarrassment, that she'd been so confident of her persuasive skills, and shame that she'd failed so miserably. But there had been other emotions, too, feelings of connection that held meaning for her, now as then—and as Spock sat on the couch beside her, it was that connection she wanted. Her pride had been wounded, but bearing him a grudge for his loyalties was nothing, less than nothing, a useless exercise in useless emotion. He'd done what he'd had to do, just as she had.

Without speaking, his careful gaze taking her in, he reached for her. His fingertips were cool and dry, nestling into her hair and resting against her brow.

He moved closer to her, his lips pressing together slightly as he adjusted his touch.

The commander closed her eyes, aware of the heat of his body, the sound of his breathing. She had to be mad, letting this happen, *asking* for it to happen, she knew it but she didn't want to put a stop to it, either.

"Relax," Spock said softly, his voice deep and soothing by its very poise. "Breathe."

She leaned against the couch's back, her eyes still closed, amazed to think that this was her reality, that he was touching her and she was willing. She expected that he knew her idea to bond was only partially for the reason she'd stated—and truly, she wouldn't feel right telling him Empire secrets without being sure of his objectives—but she also suspected that he could pluck the information from her mind if he so chose.

I do this because I wish to know him. Anything else is a pretense.

It was her last clear, focused thought.

She realized faintly that she could no longer hear his breathing, both of them inhaling and exhaling as one. There was a curious sensation of gently falling, drifting, not down but away. Toward.

"Our thoughts are as one," he said, his voice even softer, deeper, the sound like a sudden small light in total darkness, drawing her focus—and the change was so gradual, so peaceful, that she hardly noticed the transition as she slipped into his consciousness.

Distantly, she felt his fingers in her hair, through his hands. She felt a cool tide of mild thought, the careful structure beneath . . . and beneath that were emotions, but not quite as she knew them. The feelings were strangely removed, powerful but abstracted. She felt them, but it was her own perception that gave them definition. Struggle. Doubt. Regret. Love. And loneliness, so strong that she ached with it, so pervasive that it was not separate from him, from them.

These were the things that he did not allow himself, but could neither cast out. She found disdain for himself, and frustration. She found his honesty, his morality—and there she found herself, and understood.

There is no lie.

Again, the silver-blue rush of intellect, washing over it all, and she realized that she had seen things, felt things that he seldom acknowledged. The intimacy was shocking in its depth, thrilling and frightening, and she felt him trying to guide her away, to give her back to herself—but he wanted to enter her mind, too, he resisted the desire but couldn't hide it.

With great effort, she found her voice.

Feel me.

She didn't know if she spoke out loud or only thought it, but he heard her. Now, she noticed the change. Spock had opened to her slowly, cautiously, and though she understood that he was now trying to move as carefully into her own thoughts, the sensation was different, a shift of control, an acceptance—being seen instead of seeing. The restrained and gentle essence of him was moving inside of her, experiencing her, just as she had experienced him. And then there was no separation. They were one.

There was no understanding of time where they were, no awareness of physical form. She hadn't understood how vulnerable she would be to him, how dependent on him to determine and reestablish boundaries until she recognized him as distinct again, felt herself as apart. There was relief and sadness, a shared understanding of the experience as unique, singular, a recognition that their paths were dissimilar and separate. There was a sensation of drifting away . . . and then she felt her heart beating, and his fingertips pressed lightly against her temples.

When he moved his hands, she opened her eyes, watching as he backed away from her personal space, moving to a conversational distance— although for a few moments, there was nothing that needed to be said, nothing at all.

After a time, he asked her questions about the cloaking device, and she started talking.

Chapter Eleven

Except for the captain's calls, Uhura had done nothing but fuss with that stubborn and mean-spirited code for coming up on three hours straight. She'd never seen anything quite like it, and neither had the ship's computer—for all the hundreds of written symbol languages the *Enterprise* had on file, not one of them matched up to what was on the data chip any better than another.

Three symbols, single-digit number. Six symbols, two-digit number. Ten symbols, another single-digit number, and so on, pages of it. At first glance, it hadn't looked too difficult—a symbol for a letter, a number for a space . . . except there were an odd number of symbols and too many of them, even though Captain Darres's files didn't indicate that he knew any language besides English. And the symbols weren't consistent when she tried to plug in substitutes, not to *any* language she'd ever heard of.

The symbol that might represent one letter in one word didn't seem to be the same in another, and she couldn't tell where the representations changed, where they became something else. After the first two hours, she tried glaring at the screen until everything ran together, but that didn't help much, either.

Although she could have chosen to work in a more private area, she stayed at her station on the bridge, so used to tuning out distractions that her concentration was just fine. Her frustration level, though . . . she'd been at the top of her class in the Academy's code and cryptography program, but at the moment, looking at all those angular and curvy little characters in no perceivable pattern, she couldn't for the life of her remember how she'd managed to pass at all.

The numbers had to indicate where the representations change, they *had* to . . . except they didn't have to, no matter how obvious it seemed, no matter how much she wished it were so. It was deeply vexing, to have a chance to use some of her skills on something besides the every day, and then to find herself so absolutely *stuck*.

"Computer, highlight the probable vowels again," she sighed. Assuming it was English. Assuming the words weren't spelled backward, or cross-matched from a grid . . . or worse, that the code was based on a book or a writing, the numbers and symbols representing marked pages and words. Without a key, those were nearly impossible to break . . . which was why she hadn't seriously considered it, not yet. Because if that was the case, she might as well go ahead and tear her hair out now, rather than putting it off—

"Still no luck, huh? Have you tried substituting the small groupings with words like 'the' and 'and'?"

Uhura glanced up, saw Sulu looking over her shoulder.

"Yes, thank you," she said, hard-pressed to keep the irritation out of her voice. He was only trying to help.

"I was going to get some coffee," he said. "Would you like me to bring you some?"

That was *much* more helpful. She smiled gratefully. "Thank you, Sulu, that's very nice of you. Cream and sugar?"

"You got it." He squinted again at the screen, then shook his head. "It all looks the same from here, bunch of lines and squiggles."

Tell me about it.

He left, and Uhura sat back in her chair, frowning. It *did* look all the same, really. A vertical line, two curves. A curve, a slash, another curve. Four lines in a row, of different heights. It was as though someone had dropped the alphabet into a blender and poured the results out on her screen.

Uhura started to stretch, raising her arms above her head—and then froze. She dropped her hands and leaned forward, studying the characters with new intensity. There were patterns, physical patterns. Those four lines in a row were common, where a vowel might be. Where the letter "E" might be. Two curves and a line, the letter "B," maybe, and there were the same curves and lines in a different configuration—

If the letters were taken apart and put back together and if the numbers represent which letter in each group is going to change configuration, or the number of words away where the change takes place . . .

It fit, it fit and it felt right. She'd still have to figure out the numbers, *get the computer to sort characters by shape, fill in the obvious ones and then start looking at the math—*

The lieutenant smiled widely, suddenly giddy with pride. Sulu deserved a kiss; it seemed she was going to get to keep her hair, after all.

The captain was waiting in the transporter room when Scott returned to the ship, standing with his arms crossed, his impatience as plain as day. As the hum of the transporter faded, the captain was already stepping up to the platform. Scotty picked up his tool kit, sighing. As glad as he was to be back on the ship, he wasn't particularly looking forward to their conversation.

"Well, Mr. Scott?"

"Sir, I didn't find anything you could call real evidence, exactly—but I didn't *not* find anything, either."

"Explain," the captain snapped.

Aye, he was in a mood. Scotty put the tool kit back down, and saw Tam shoot a sympathetic look in his direction from behind the transporter console. Scott ignored it, though he made a mental note to later remind young Mr. Tam that he should pay mind to his own business.

"Well, I checked Captain Darres's temporary quarters, like you asked," Scotty said. "Did a real

thorough job of it, too—I went over every square
centimeter with the tricorder, looking for variations
of density and temperature in the walls, floor, and
ceiling. I scanned the furniture, his personals—even
a bottle of Saurian brandy I came across, all of it for
any sign at all that something was amiss. There was
no bug, sir, I would've found it . . . but I *did* find evidence that someone has been at the ventilator duct in
there. The vent's grating had been pried out of place,
and recently; the tiny scratches in the alloy had
barely begun the oxidation process."

The captain was plainly unimpressed by the information, giving it a perfunctory nod. "Nothing we
can use. What about the transporters?"

"Again, there'd be nothing I could prove, one way
or another," Scott said. "There was nothing tangible,
you understand—"

"I understand," Captain Kirk said briskly. "What
didn't you not find in the transporter system?"

"My diagnostic matched up to theirs," Scott
sighed. "The malfunction was due to a stray irregu-
larity in the autosequencing program—a one-in-a-
billion mishap, and only dangerous in about ten
percent of those cases. It's probably the most common reason for transporter fatalities, though you're
still looking at a very small number . . . but it does
happen every now and again.

"The thing is, I decided to open up the control
console, just to take a look, you know, give her a
once-over, scan the phase-transition coils and the
like—and at the very highest tricorder setting for
field readings, I picked up what could be evidence of
a directed magnetic pulse."

The captain was frowning. "Which means . . ."

"If I was looking to get rid of someone using a transporter without raising any eyebrows, that's how I'd do it, sir," Scott said. "One tap on a standard magnetic generator, set for a specific range and quality—and they make them no bigger than a communicator, mind you—and you've got one dead man. It would only affect a single trip, too, so there'd be no chance of killing another."

"That's it, it has to be," Kirk said, seeming both agitated and excited by the discovery—which made Scott all the more reluctant to tell him the rest of it.

"Sir, I said it *could* be a magnetic pulse," he said heavily. "Unfortunately, with as weak as the trace was, it could also be about a dozen other things, most of them caused by natural emissions from an overused system—and with that conference going on, the station's transporters have had plenty of use lately. There's just no way to tell for sure."

The captain sighed. "I don't suppose there were any security monitors in or near that transporter room, either."

"No, Captain. Nary a one."

"What about M-20's investigation? Did you talk to the station manager?"

Here was the kicker. Scotty braced himself, fully aware that it was going to go over like a lead balloon.

"Aye, I talked to him. Mr. Miatsu walked me to the scene himself. Station security has already interviewed everyone—the guard who escorted Captain Darres to the transporters, and the young man who ran the controls, as well as a few others working in the area. It seemed it all happened just after a shift change, and with the summit and all, there were a few minutes that the room was empty and no one was watching . . . but without any evidence . . ."

Scotty took a deep breath. "The manager told me that unless something else turned up, he was going to have to rule Captain Darres's death an accident. He said he'd send you the report as soon as he was done with it."

Although he'd expected an angry response, Captain Kirk only shook his head. He looked frustrated and unhappy, but somehow not a bit surprised by the news.

"Captain, do you know what's happening?" Scott asked. "Is it something to do with Captain Darres's looking into the *Sphinx* misfortune?"

"I don't know anything for sure, not yet," the captain said grimly, looking at Scott but not seeing him, his expression troubled and deeply thoughtful. "But something's going on . . . and I'm starting to think that whatever it is, it's a lot bigger than we know."

He focused on the engineer again, reaching out to clap him on the shoulder. "You did a good job, Mr. Scott."

"Thank you, sir," Scotty said, proud as always when the captain acknowledged his hard work.

"Bridge to Captain Kirk." Lieutenant Uhura's voice.

The captain stepped to the intercom. "Kirk here."

"Captain, I've managed to decipher the data chip." Uhura's pretty voice was as efficient as always, but Scott thought she also sounded thoroughly pleased with herself.

"Excellent, Lieutenant. I'm on my way, Kirk out."

With a nod at Scotty, and Mr. Tam at the transporter controls, the captain headed off to the bridge looking a wee bit more hopeful than he had only a moment before. Mr. Scott was glad to see it. The afternoon he'd spent at the station had been an uncomfortable one, looking for proof that a Starfleet captain had been watched and murdered. It was enough to drive a man to drink, but if it was true, the captain would get to the bottom of it . . . and if he thought that some data chip would shed light on the matter, maybe it would at that.

Gladly putting the whole sorry business out of mind, Scott turned a sharp eye toward Mr. Tam to give him a few words about good manners.

The expression on Chekov's face when he walked into sickbay made McCoy's heart sink. The boy looked undone, pale and bleak, and McCoy was suddenly absolutely certain that Karen Patterson was dead. She was dead, and his hope was dead along with her.

"Why hello, Mr. Chekov," Nurse Chapel said brightly. She was at the counter, sorting through the second to last batch of physical test results. "Is something the matter?"

Chekov managed to smile, but it was a weak affair. "No, ma'am. Dr. McCoy, may I speak to you privately for a moment?"

"Of course," McCoy said, his voice far away to his own ears. He hoped that Christine would mistake his dread for concern. "We can talk in the recovery room."

Chekov followed him, practically stepping on

his heels he was so anxious. Whatever it was, it was bad.

As soon as the door closed behind them, McCoy turned to face the young navigator, bracing himself for the worst. It had been a long shot, anyway.

"Doctor, I found something—I didn't think I was going to at first, she was hard to pick up after she left Altair VI, but I tracked her down," Chekov said rapidly, and even as obviously distressed as he was, McCoy could hear a trace of pride in his statement, the accent on "I."

Maybe she's not dead after all. Chekov certainly wasn't acting like someone delivering bad news. A spark of hope rekindled.

"After Altair she took some time off, that's what made it difficult, there were no records for six months," Chekov continued. "But then she got a research job with a medical chemical company in the Tellun star system, a division of the Carter Winston Group. She was there until just two months ago, when she suddenly resigned and booked passage to Deep Space Station R-5. Her and a half-dozen other Federation doctors met there from all over, very important people, I saw the arrival logs."

"So, is that where she is now?" McCoy asked.

"No, sir," the young man replied, his eyes wide. "A ship picked her up from R-5 only a day later, and the others, and not one of them has turned up anywhere else. It's like they all just disappeared into thin air."

McCoy shook his head, confused and thoroughly irritated, but before he could say anything, Chekov spilled the rest.

"Doctor, the ship that picked them up was the *Sphinx,* Jack Casden commanding."

McCoy just stared at him for a moment, speechless, until Chekov started babbling nervously about how they had to tell the captain. In spite of his shock, McCoy somehow managed to assure Chekov that he would take care of it, not to worry and not to talk about it to anyone else. Having shared the burden of knowledge, the navigator calmed down and wanted to talk about the unlikely coincidence, but McCoy made an excuse to get rid of him, thanked him and sent him along his way.

McCoy sat down on one of the diagnostic beds, thinking. He needed to decide what to tell Jim . . . and it was time he got caught up on what had been happening since he'd stopped paying attention to ship's business, because it appeared that his personal business was about to become a part of it. After a few minutes, he got up and went to see if he could find those station arrival logs Chekov had been talking about, wondering if he would know when it was time for him to stop hoping.

Chapter Twelve

The death of Captain Darres was most regrettable, the more so because it was highly doubtful that it had been an accident . . . although Spock also considered it doubtful that a murderous intent would ever be proved.

Spock was informed of Darres's demise upon his return to M-20, by an ensign who had been a part of the *Sphinx* investigation team. It seemed that the ensign and the other members of the team actually believed that a transporter malfunction was responsible. Spock made no attempt to dissuade them, primarily because he wished to return to the *Enterprise* and speak to the captain, but also because it now seemed that the overly knowledgeable had become exceedingly short-lived.

After his extensive conversation with the Romulan commander about cloaking technology, Spock felt that he had enough information to present a theory to the captain. Not a complete one, there were still a number of unknowns, but he believed he'd reached a workable premise from which to take action.

The captain was in his quarters when Spock beamed back to the *Enterprise*. Spock decided to go to him rather than ask to be met, as he believed that the death of the captain's friend and former shipmate had likely taken an emotional toll.

As he left the transporter room and started for the captain's quarters, Spock considered some of the unknown factors they still faced. He felt reasonably certain that Dr. Kettaract was using cloaking technology for his own designs, and that he had obtained the technology from his study of the device that Starfleet Intelligence held. Spock had reached the conclusion after the commander had informed him that only the single cloaking device, the one that he and the captain had taken from her ship, had ever been lost by the Romulan Empire. However, he still did not know what Dr. Kettaract was trying to keep hidden, or who else was involved.

There was also the specific nature of the *Sphinx*'s involvement. It seemed logical that the fatalities of Captain Casden and his crew were caused by their discovery of Dr. Kettaract's machinations; the abrupt death of Captain Darres certainly supported the theory . . . but how they had discovered the doctor's plan was still unclear. The possibility that they had stumbled across it by chance seemed unlikely. And if the unidentified man on the *Sphinx* was responsible for that ship's doom, who had killed Captain Darres?

"Spock, wait up!"

Spock turned and saw Dr. McCoy hurrying down the corridor. He held a piece of paper in one hand, and by his posture and expression seemed quite anxious.

"Are you going to see Jim?" the doctor asked, upon reaching him. A logical assumption; his quarters were just around the next turn.

"Yes, Doctor."

"So am I," the doctor said, uncharacteristically amiable. "I found something that might have to do with the *Sphinx*—well, technically Chekov found it. I asked him for a favor, I wanted help looking for this old friend of mine, and it just turned up."

Spock cocked an eyebrow. "I'm sure the story behind this discovery is most exciting, Doctor. Apparently more so than the discovery itself."

The doctor made a familiar, thunderous face. "That's what I get for trying to tell *you* anything. Look, it turns out that this friend of mine, she's a doctor, and a few other top-notch research scientists and the like disappeared not so long ago, after they were picked up by the *Sphinx*." He held up the piece of paper. "Seven in all."

Highly intriguing. "May I see that, Doctor?"

Dr. McCoy handed him a list of the missing scientists' names . . . and after reading them, it was clear that at least two of the unexplained elements of his hypothesis now had to be recategorized.

"Doctor, I believe we need to speak with the captain immediately," Spock said, and as it occasionally happened, Dr. McCoy did not disagree.

Kirk sat staring at the monitor, hoping to God that he was wrong, vaguely wishing for his earlier feelings of frustration and discouragement.

He *had* been frustrated after Uhura showed him what she'd uncovered. The coded data chip, the thing that was supposed to clear up the mystery, that was going to explain everything, had turned out to be nothing more than a copy of the Starfleet Charter. It was in the files of every ship and every starbase. And after taking it back to his quarters for a quick, hopeful scan, searching for concealed messages, he'd felt on the verge of giving up. No evidence, no answers, no progress, a ship and her crew destroyed, his friend and mentor dead. His unofficial investigation was officially dead in the water, and unless Spock had something up his sleeve, Kirk didn't know how to move forward.

Still, Darres had coded the thing for a reason. With nothing better to do, Kirk cued it back to the beginning and read, searching every sentence for some hidden meaning, feeling his disappointment slowly and steadily gather strength . . . until he found it. Found something, anyway.

Deeply troubled, he was still gazing blankly at the monitor when someone signaled at his door. Without thinking about it, Kirk snapped the monitor off before inviting his visitor in.

Two visitors. Spock and McCoy came in together.

"How was your trip, Mr. Spock?" Kirk asked,

forcing what he'd seen in the Charter out of his mind.

For now.

"Successful, Captain," Spock said. "Between my discussion with the Romulan commander and the information I've just received from Dr. McCoy, I believe I now understand the connection between Dr. Kettaract and what happened to Captain Casden's ship and crew, as well as to Captain Darres. And if I'm correct, we may have very little time in which to act."

Bones was scowling. "Then why don't you spit it out?"

"I am attempting to do so, Doctor, and if you will allow me to—"

"Knock it off," Kirk snapped. "Spock, report."

"My hypothesis is this," Spock said calmly. "The *Sphinx* was sabotaged by someone attempting to prevent it from leaving the Lantaru sector, where there is an illegally cloaked Federation station. There, Dr. Bendes Kettaract is leading a team of scientists in an attempt to synthesize an Omega molecule, the same energy source he postulated early in his career, which theory indicates will not maintain stabilization and is therefore exceedingly dangerous. Captain Casden probably learned of the cloak when he transported part of Kettaract's science team from Deep Space Station R-5 to the Lantaru station, approximately two months ago.

"It appears that the *Sphinx* traveled to the Lantaru station several times, Casden operating under the belief that his orders were from Starfleet Intelligence and highly classified—but that at some point, he recognized them as fraudulent and decided to disclose Dr. Kettaract's work and location to Starfleet.

"I believe that he confronted Dr. Kettaract at the cloaked station, and that Dr. Kettaract arranged for the sabotage of the *Sphinx*. The deaths of Jack Casden and his crew may have been accidental. Dr. Kettaract's work is nearing completion; therefore, he only meant for the *Sphinx* to be lost for a brief period, long enough for a planted rumor to taint Casden's credibility, so that his claims would not immediately be believed.

"From the evidence, there are a number of unidentified people supporting Dr. Kettaract's work. At least one of them willing to kill to maintain its secrecy, as is evidenced by the allegedly accidental death of Gage Darres. I believe it likely that a careful network of misinformation, built by an unscrupulous few, has even made unwitting participants of Starfleet officers."

My God.

Bones looked just as stunned as Kirk felt, the complexities astounding, the repercussions frightening—that all those people might have died just so an obsessed scientist could indulge his paranoia. Some of it was a total surprise, but because Spock was the one telling him, Kirk didn't waste time on disbelief.

"Why do you think he's working on Omega?" Kirk asked.

"Because of his history, and because of who he has most recently chosen to work with his team. Medical theorists and mechanical engineers, primarily, who will study the physical effects of his creation and begin seeking ways to employ its power."

"Why the rush?" Bones asked. "How do we know he's really that close?"

"Because he believes that he is," Spock said simply. "And because of the message that he received last night, from someone named Hermes. The importance that was placed on the first name, John instead of Tom—I believe it was a code. In Earth mythology, Hermes was the messenger of the gods. I don't know the significance of the first names, but I suspect 'John' meant that they were to return to the station immediately. Presumably because the experiment has reached a crucial stage."

They.

"And considering the possible consequences if he should actually achieve synthesis," Spock continued, "it is incumbent upon us to stop them as soon as is possible."

"How serious are we talking about?" Kirk asked.

"A precise classification is not possible, as the molecule has never existed," Spock said. "The result of the inevitable destabilization may only be the destruction of the station itself . . . but depending on their containment methods, it is conceivable that an expanding energy field could form in subspace, severely damaging that continuum within an indefinite but possibly extensive range."

Kirk hesitated only a second, just long enough to absorb the immensity of what Spock was suggesting, to calculate whether or not they could beat Kettaract—

—and Jain, amazing, beautiful Jain—

—back to his station. Probably not, but they could come damned close.

He thumbed the intercom switch.

"Kirk to engineering. Mr. Scott, get the engines ready. We're going back to the Lantaru sector, and we're going to need warp eight."

Chapter Thirteen

Suni had suspected that some of the other doctors at the station were getting cold feet, she'd seen it coming for weeks, so she was prepared for a hitch or two when they finally docked. In between yearning thoughts of Jim and her own excitement—they were literally hours from synthesis—she'd spent most of the trip home coaching Bendes on how to handle it.

As soon as they boarded the station, stepping into the cool, antiseptic-scented brightness of what had once been a cargo bay, she saw that it was more serious than she'd figured. Most of the team was waiting to greet them, excited and impatient for the culmination of their hard work, but there were six conspicuous absences.

"Welcome home, Doctors!"

John Connolly was wearing a huge grin, much bigger than his brother's, standing next to him. Tom Connolly had been betting all along that the pressurized chemical vat prep would be a total failure, a bet that his younger brother had taken him up on. It had been Suni's idea to use their names as signals, on the off chance that the station needed to contact them at the summit.

"John, not Tom," Kettaract said, smiling. "What did you win?"

"It's not what he won, it's what I lost," Tom said good-naturedly. "Top billing in the history books to my younger brother, thank you very much."

Every one of the sixteen assembled scientists and technicians laughed, a sound of barely suppressed jubilance, the very air electric with a sense of gleeful accomplishment. She was glad to see them so excited, they deserved it. A few of them had been with Kettaract since the very beginning, when he'd been working out of an abandoned warehouse on a non-aligned planet in the Taugan sector. Before he'd met the people she worked for.

"Where are the others?" Kettaract asked.

"Cafeteria," John said, his smile fading slightly. "When they realized how close we are ... it's not that they don't believe in you, Bendes, they're just scared."

"Now that it's actually happening, I think they just can't believe it," Wesker piped up, sniffing loudly. The physicist seemed to have a perpetually runny nose. "It's a kind of denial. Fear of success."

Suni had to smile. Success in this case meant fame and fortune, while failure likely meant death; she doubted very much that they were terribly afraid of succeeding. The problem was faith, as it had been all along. Faith in Bendes, faith in themselves.

"I believe I could use one last meal before we forever change the course of history," Kettaract said, initiating more laughter. "Let's all go. I have a few things I want to say, to everyone."

The group broke into couples and trios as they trooped out into the station's interior, chatting happily at each other. Suni hung back a little, watching them. It was amazing to see, after so many months, *years,* of knowing them as pale, solemn people, always with clipboards in hand, always frowning.

I probably looked the same way, skulking around this cavernous, empty station with no real life, calculating and recalculating the probabilities over and over. . . .

Not anymore, not ever again. She'd done her part, as a scientist and as a motivator—running equations, keeping her contacts informed, teaching Bendes how to inspire his team. Taking care of problems. When the cloak had become available, she'd been the one to talk him into it, pointing out how close they were, how they couldn't afford to be interrupted.

She had kept the project going, all in the name of making the Federation into what it should be. With the power of the Omega molecule backing it up, there would be nothing to stand in the way, nothing to keep the Federation from its altruistic goals— uniting all worlds, creating peace and prosperity for every living being who wanted to be a part of it.

Not a bad way to have spent her time . . . but she was exhausted, tired of accepting the harsh responsibility for so many of the setbacks and mistakes, tired of carrying Bendes and the others through their tantrums and doubts.

Let's not forget the loneliness, Jain, her mind whispered cruelly, *all those days and weeks and months of secrets.* She didn't need a reminder; it wasn't possible to forget. Not even Kettaract knew who she really was.

But after tonight, everything changed. There'd be a few weeks of initial research before they officially went public . . . which meant she'd be able to get away for a week or two while the med docs and engineers started in, to take a real break. There was no way anyone would begrudge her that.

A week or two with Jim Kirk, she hoped—fulfilling the promise of that lingering kiss, definitely, but she thought there could be more. It would be a chance to find out . . . and even if nothing lasting came from it, she wasn't going to be worrying about having wasted her time, relaxing with an attractive, strong, honest man, maybe even telling him a few of her less compromising secrets. The irony really was something, considering his part in collecting the cloaking device that concealed the project. . . . not that he ever needed to know about *that.*

But I could talk about my work on the molecule. He's Starfleet, he'd be thrilled. In another hour or two, it wouldn't really matter if the truth got out about Kettaract's work. It just meant there'd be more people glorying in their success.

The renewed thought of what was about to happen made her heart pound. As she followed the others into the cafeteria, she could barely resist a sudden urge to dance. It was happening, it was finally happening.

The six scientists who were already sitting in the

cafeteria were grouped together anxiously, huddled over cups of coffee. They watched their colleagues march in with carefully neutral expressions, but they couldn't hide their body language, the rounded shoulders, the lowered heads. Suni felt sorry for them; if she had any doubt that Bendes Kettaract could pull it off, she'd be scared, too.

"Everyone, take a seat, please," Kettaract said, walking toward the front of the room. "I'd like to say a few words."

Suni silently willed him to remember at least some of her extensive advice. It should be fine, he was in too good a mood to go off on one of his tears, as he'd done only the night before. She still couldn't believe that he'd been stupid enough to draw so much attention to himself, without even knowing how close they were to finishing.

Anyway, he can hardly screw up. Everyone here wants to believe.

"It appears that tonight's the night," he said, smiling widely. A few people applauded. "And it seems appropriate for me to stand up and tell you all how proud I am, that each of you is here with me, now. I know it hasn't always been easy, but you stuck it out; you studied the work, you saw its integrity . . . and you made sacrifices in your own lives to come here, to live and work with me on my dream. And that's made it your dream, too."

Sounds like he actually listened for a change. He'd touched on the solidity of his work, added a note of humility and an acknowledgment that they'd all suffered a little. Exactly as she'd suggested.

"I realize that there's some concern out there,

some nervousness," he continued, "and I think that's only natural. The awesome power of Omega is nothing to take lightly . . . but neither is the importance of what we're doing here. Is there a risk? Of course, though we all know that it's infinitesimal. But changing the course of history . . . well, that's a risky business. And I believe, absolutely, that we are about to get a huge payoff for taking a very small chance.

"We are about to create a universe of possibility for our children, and our children's children . . . for the future of every Federation citizen. Peace, forever."

He had them, the doubters. Suni could see it in Kaylor's eyes, in Patterson's face, in the way Angelo was puffing out his chest. It was exactly what they needed to hear.

Kettaract smiled, shaking his head. "Look at me, making speeches. All I really wanted to do was say thank you, so . . . thank you. And thanks for listening."

More applause, laughter, shouted you're-welcomes. If Suni didn't know better, she might actually think he was a humble man; he hadn't bothered mentioning that in private he referred to most of them as lackeys, insisting that only a handful were actually competent . . . but then, that probably wouldn't set the right tone for Kettaract's big day.

Suni liked several people on the station. She'd taken pride in the work she'd done to contribute to Kettaract's molecule, and she believed deeply in the ultimate objective, giving the Federation the power it deserved . . . but at the moment, tonight was all that mattered, and all that she really cared about. She'd been teamed with Bendes Kettaract to get results, and after nearly three years of hard work, she was finally going to prevail.

She was still thinking as much when she saw Dickerson motioning at her from the doorway. Kubaro Dickerson headed up the small group who kept the station's essentials running, and was the only other person on board sent by the experiment's supporters since Max had gone.

As soon as she reached him, he pulled her into the hall. He was uncharacteristically nervous, his expression worried, a small tic at the corner of his left eye.

"There's a ship out there," he said, keeping his voice low.

Instantly, Suni's happiness dried up. "What? Federation? How close?"

"Starfleet, Constitution-class," he said. "It's about eight hundred million kilometers out, but it looks like they're headed in this direction."

"No problems with the cloak?"

Dickerson shook his head. "No—but what the hell are they doing out here?"

Suni didn't answer. She was too busy mentally cursing Kettaract for his inflammatory rant back at the summit, practically begging for Starfleet to check him out.

It seemed that somebody had decided to take him up on it.

McCoy postponed the last of the crew physicals for a day, knowing that he was too preoccupied to do a good job. He paced sickbay instead, not sure what he should do.

If Spock's theory was right—and his theories almost always were, confound him—Karen Patterson had hooked up with a rogue group of geniuses, convinced that they were going to change the universe. McCoy knew Jim well enough to know that he'd put a stop to their Omega experiment, one way or another . . . but what about Karen? How obsessed was she with what she was working on, what if she wasn't interested in helping someone she'd barely known in med school?

And how am I supposed to get hold of her to find out?

Jim had been pretty vague about plans, beyond finding the station. The idea was to trace the *Sphinx's* recorded trajectory back into the Lantaru sector, and then look for recent particle exhaust from Kettaract's ship. Assuming they could even find the damned station, assuming that the scientists on board didn't try to escape when they realized they were found out, what then? Depending on how many people were involved, the *Enterprise* would either take Dr. Kettaract and his people into custody, or stand guard until a bigger transport ship could arrive . . . but either way, Karen Patterson was probably going to end up in a penitentiary somewhere, and it seemed pretty unlikely that any of those places maintained disease-research facilities.

For about the millionth time since he'd been diagnosed, McCoy felt a surge of guilt, for worrying about himself over everything else, for considering practically everything by how it related to him, to curing his xenopolycythemia. He couldn't seem to help it. It was either that, or . . .

. . . or face death. Accept that you're going to die.

He wasn't ready, and he wasn't about to give up, not when there was still a chance. When he realized that the ship had dropped out of warp, he headed straight for the bridge.

Everyone was at their stations, the viewscreen showing a big, empty nothing, as expected. McCoy moved to stand behind Jim's chair, gazing out at the expanse of blackness and stars.

"Anything?" Jim asked.

Spock was bent over his sensors. "Negative. I don't—"

He broke off, adjusting a knob on the side of his directed console. "Captain, I'm picking up matter-antimatter particle exhaust bearing one one seven mark seven."

"Slow and steady, Mr. Sulu," Jim said, absently rubbing at his lower lip with the fingertips of his left hand, staring at the screen as though he expected to see something.

McCoy did the very same, and wondered if Karen was out there in the dark, staring back at them and wishing they would go away.

Chapter Fourteen

Kirk watched the screen as the *Enterprise* edged deeper into the Lantaru sector, thinking about their next move.

Spock had found traces of a postwarp vent, what had to be Kettaract's ship, but it was dissipating fast—and even if they managed to stop right next to the station, Kirk couldn't think of a nonviolent way to force them to decloak. No one would be able to transport over, though he supposed they could send over some kind of recorded message . . . he didn't know about reasoning with Kettaract, but if he could get to Jain, he knew she would see sense.

If she has any say in the matter. She was smart, but Kettaract might have duped her into believing that everything was safe . . . just as he might have sabotaged the *Sphinx* without her knowing. He knew it was wishful thinking, but he also honestly couldn't imagine her hurting anybody.

"Adjust to one two zero mark five," Spock said.

"Yes sir," Sulu acknowledged, watching his console.

"So what are you planning to do, exactly?" Bones asked, stepping forward to stand at Kirk's right. "Just fly around until we run into them?"

Kirk didn't answer McCoy's sardonic question, his mind going back to the idea of transporting an object through the cloak. It seemed like the best way to contact the station, and certainly the safest. The problem was not knowing the exact coordinates—and even if they got lucky, managed to drop a tricorder or clipboard into an open area on the station, they could end up beaming it into somebody's closet, somewhere no one would find it. The graviton field made finding life signs impossible; the energy output from the cloaking device was so great that it obscured all direct sensor readings, except for the existence of the gravitons themselves. Even then you had to be looking for them in a specific pattern, and all you'd end up finding if you tried to trace it was—

Of course. The thought was a revelation, the plan instantly in place. If Spock could find it, and Scotty could intensify a transporter beam high enough—

"Spock—using the graviton patterns that Mr. Scott recorded, would it be possible to zero in on the source? On the cloaking device itself?"

Spock straightened, an expression of intense deliberation on his face as he turned to look at Kirk.

"Yes," he said slowly, frowning. "I see . . . assuming the facility is stationary. But transporting it would take an immense amount of energy . . ."

Kirk felt a flash of triumph at Spock's response. If Mr. Spock said it was possible, it was possible—and if the power existed, Scotty would find a way to make it happen.

"Full stop, Mr. Sulu, and stand by," Kirk said, reaching for the intercom. They'd never know what hit them.

Half an hour. If they could just stay hidden for another half hour, everything would be ready and it wouldn't matter anymore.

If there's a God, just give us a few more minutes, please, Suni thought as she hurried to the lab. The starship was less than fifteen thousand kilometers away and closing; there was no question in her mind that having lost the transport's signature—the only way they could have made it this close—they were sitting there scanning for unusual readings. She had nightmarish visions of the Starfleet vessel shooting a probe into what they saw as an anomaly, maybe directing a charged beam into it and destroying them all, either by directly hitting them hard enough to breach the hull or accidentally tripping off some of the potentially deadly chemicals and equipment they had around.

Kettaract was overseeing the final calibrations to the accelerators, double-checking the photo-multiplier tubes, running back and forth and probably making a huge nuisance of himself when she arrived. She understood his excitement, but he was slowing things up. Until it was time to flip the last switch for the countdown—and the honor was rightfully his—his presence wasn't required in the lab . . . and when he heard about the ship, he was going to go from being a hassle to being a raving, shouting distraction that they absolutely could not afford.

Please, God, give us a break, I'll never ask for anything ever again.

Determined not to disrupt anyone's concentration at such a crucial time, Suni pulled Kettaract toward the door, telling him she needed just a moment to discuss something—

—and before they'd gone two steps, the red-alert panels in the lab started to blink and caterwaul, the alarms resounding through the vast, open space and sounding like the end of the universe. And even through the surprised cries of the scientists and technicians, through her own racing, panicked thoughts and the absolute horror dawning on Kettaract's face, she realized, deep down, that either God didn't exist or that He absolutely hated her guts.

At the helm, Sulu watched the screen closely, wondering what was going to happen. Was a space station suddenly going to appear, like some photographic effect? Or would there be a few seconds, a kind of fading-in while the cloaking device was being transported?

Or will it work at all? So far as he knew, nothing like this had ever been tried before.

The intercom was open, Mr. Spock continuing to narrow the search while Mr. Scott carefully adjusted coordinates, the captain's clever idea slowly becoming a reality. In front of the ship there was only endless space, and though he tried to discern some sign, some blur or ripple that would give the cloaked station away, Sulu couldn't see a thing. It was eerie, thinking that there might be hundreds of people just sitting out there, silently watching . . .

"Captain, I've narrowed it to one square meter of the highest graviton density," Mr. Spock said. "I will not be able to reduce the area any further."

"Then that will just have to be close enough," Captain Kirk replied. "Let's hope no one's standing next to it, or they're going to get one hell of a surprise."

"Mr. Scott, please readjust the ACB to eleven billion parts per millimeter," Spock said, "and lock coordinates."

"Aye," the engineer responded. "I've got her in my sights; just say the word."

Sulu tried not to blink. It seemed like he could actually feel the intense scrutiny of everyone on the bridge, everyone staring at the main screen, waiting for the captain's signal.

"Energize."

Sulu hadn't even realized that he was holding his breath until a gasp was forced out of him, as a dark, massive wall blocked out most of the stars, instantly, extending away from them for what seemed like forever before curving out of sight. This close the *Enterprise* was dwarfed by it, a flea on a dog's back, its sudden, looming appearance a frightening surprise.

Everyone on the bridge reacted, Uhura even letting out a soft *oh*, but the captain didn't blink.

"Scotty, I take it we have a cloaking device," he said calmly, nodding at the helm. "Go to fifty percent magnification."

Chekov shakily reached for the controls as Mr. Scott responded, a grin in his voice. "Aye, sir. And a goodly piece of a shield-generator console, too."

A second later the screen blinked and they could see it in its entirety, an immense wheel-shaped station tilted about twenty degrees at its axis. It was a design Sulu had never seen before, the angle and the dark, metallic hull giving it a strangely menacing appearance.

Well, and the fact that it popped up like a monster from under a kid's bed certainly doesn't add to its appeal.

"Lieutenant, open a channel," the captain said. "See if either Dr. Bendes Kettaract or Dr. Jain Suni is available to speak to us about their experiment."

If Captain Kirk was pleased at all with the success of his plan, he wasn't showing it. He seemed almost unhappy, in fact, though Sulu couldn't imagine why.

Someone had turned off the alarms, at least, and while Kettaract attempted to calm everyone down, Jain tried desperately to think of a plan. According to Dickerson, the cloaking device was gone. She had no idea how the starship had figured it out, but there it was; they'd lost an invaluable piece of equipment and invited a possibly hostile investigation. Except it wouldn't matter one damned bit if they could just complete the synthesis.

All we have to do is keep them out for a little while, tell them . . . come on, think, you're supposed to be good at this!

Tell them we have a quarantine. Something nasty and infectious.

It would work. She couldn't imagine that any Starfleet captain would want to risk exposing his crew to a disease, and she wasn't needed in the lab; she could go talk to whoever, cough a few times and spout off something vague about a secret Intelligence project to explain the cloak. It wouldn't hold up for long, but it didn't have to. By the time they started asking the hard questions, the countdown would have already started.

Her communicator beeped. She flipped it open as she started walking toward Kettaract, to tell him to keep things moving while she handled it.

"Dr. Suni, this is Chris up in ops." Chris Bianchi, one of Dickerson's people. He sounded extremely tense. "There's someone hailing us from the *U.S.S. Enterprise*—"

Jain froze.

"—and they're asking for you by name, you or Dr. Kettaract. They actually said they wanted to talk to you about the experiment. What should I tell them?"

She didn't, couldn't answer. It was Jim out there.

How, I was so careful—

Had he followed *her?* Had it been she, not Kettaract, who'd dared Starfleet to step in by what she'd said, how she'd acted?

Didn't matter, didn't, she had to think of something, they couldn't give up now. If only there was some way she could make him understand—

As quickly as that, she had it. It wasn't foolproof, but if it worked . . . oh, God, if it worked, not only would Kettaract's molecule become the miracle it was destined to be, there was actually a chance she might end up with Jim on her side.

"Tell them to stand by," she said, and went to talk to Kettaract.

Dr. Kettaract was an older man with a shifty look about him. Chekov knew immediately, the second his smiling, disingenuous face came up on the main screen, that he was *not* a quality individual.

"Captain Kirk, isn't it? And I see Mr. Spock is with you . . . I'm Bendes Kettaract."

"I know who you are," the captain said sternly. "And I know what you're doing. This Omega molecule of yours is dangerous, Doctor, and I'm afraid I can't allow you to continue. I'm also going to have to take you and your team into custody, to face whatever charges Starfleet Intelligence sees fit to bring about."

You tell him, Captain, Chekov thought. This was probably the man responsible for murdering the crew of the *Sphinx,* and after using them to steal away Dr. McCoy's woman. He deserved no sympathy, not a bit.

Kettaract shook his head. "I don't understand— where did you get the idea that Omega is dangerous?"

Mr. Spock stepped forward. "Sir, your molecule cannot exist. It will destabilize immediately upon synthesis."

Dr. Kettaract's true colors showed for just a second, a flash of intense anger in his eyes before he was back to his insincere smile. Like the famous Russian story about the wolf in sheep's clothing.

"I disagree, Mr. Spock. From my original work, yes, I can see why you might think so—but I assure you, it has evolved through the years. And I can prove it to you, if you'll just give me a chance. I want to invite you and your captain to beam over and see all that we've accomplished, how close we are . . ."

He nodded at the captain. ". . . and I know that Dr. Suni would be more than happy to talk about what this will mean for the Federation. Believe me, Captain—everything we're doing is to further the Federation's interests."

"Does that include killing Jack Casden and his crew?" The captain asked heatedly. "Do lies and murder further the Federation's interests?"

The doctor hesitated before speaking. "That was a terrible accident," he said finally, so solemnly that Chekov almost believed him. "You have no idea how sorry I am about what happened to Captain Casden. And I'm willing to talk about going with you to the authorities, to accept my part—but not until you let me prove to you that what I'm working on here is not only possible, it's about to become reality."

Kettaract shifted his attention to Spock again. "We are literally just minutes from completion, Mr. Spock. If I can't prove to you that it's safe, I'll pack my things without a fight. But if I can . . ." The doctor smiled brilliantly, his first genuine smile of the entire conversation. "If I can, I hope you'll all stand with us, to bear witness to the birth of a new era for the Federation, and for the universe as we know it."

Right. I'll be sure to put that on my calendar. He shot a quick look at Sulu, who shot the same look right back. It seemed the doctor had been wandering around on the steppes for too long without a hat.

"Stand by," Kirk said, and Uhura automatically blanked the screen. "Mr. Spock?"

"I will admit to a certain curiosity, Captain. And we'd be able to keep him from continuing his work while we're there."

"I'd like to tag along, too, if you don't mind," Dr. McCoy said, and Chekov silently applauded when the captain agreed. It seemed that the doctor was going to see his lady friend, after all.

Hope he has better luck than I did with Joanna. Not only had she beaten him at chess, she'd announced her engagement over his fallen king. He'd had to congratulate her twice.

The captain nodded at Uhura, and Dr. Kettaract came back on screen.

"We accept your offer, Doctor."

Kettaract beamed. "You won't be sorry."

The captain called Mr. Scott up to take command, and then he and the doctor and Mr. Spock left the bridge, off to see about the false and possibly crazy doctor and his unstable experiment.

Chapter Fifteen

"How much longer?" Suni asked, watching Wesker sniffle at the computer screen, adjusting the meson reads for about the twentieth time. He was a whiz at calibrating for top and bottom quark pairs, but he was easily the slowest member of the team.

"Look at the vertical axis," Wesker said. "The pion number is still off. Spectrum needs to be broader."

Suni gritted her teeth but didn't say a word, stepping back to give him room. Everything else was ready, the team had pushed and the lab was prepped; if anything went wrong because she'd rushed the ion concentration, she'd never forgive herself.

All of the scientists were waiting, some of them already gathering at the clear plexi observation room at the front of the lab where the synthesis would take place. The others were milling around, talking in low voices. The earlier festive air was gone, which was surely best; they could celebrate later, when the molecule was secure in its containment field and all was right with the world.

Her communicator signaled. She already knew who it was and what he was going to say, but hearing it out loud made her stomach go fluttery.

"They're on their way," Dickerson said.

Of course they were. She hadn't doubted for a moment that Jim would accept Kettaract's invitation, not after what she'd told Kettaract to say about her wanting to talk. She'd been betting that whatever Jim thought of her now, whatever he *knew* exactly, he wouldn't be satisfied until he heard it from her. And it seemed she'd been right.

She turned, walked slowly toward the synthesis setup, seeing it as if for the first time—the well-spaced equipment, the scintillators waiting to be lit, acceleration rings waiting to be injected. It was going to be beautiful in its precision. Once Kettaract hit the switch, the computer would take over, faultlessly measuring the ion ratios before sending the beams through the rings. When the painstakingly perfect beams had accelerated to just the right speed, they'd be released to slam together, meeting inside the magnetic field in the center of the room that would contain the final result. A specialized energy spectrum monitor would kick on the instant the ion beams met, venting the tremendous excess of energy from the chain reaction into subspace, where it could expand harmlessly.

For the first time since hearing that a starship was outside, Suni felt like they were going to pull it off, that everything was going to work out. By inviting Jim and Mr. Spock to see how things were for themselves, to let them question Dr. Kettaract's work and get solid answers, they'd have no choice but to support it. And once the Federation actually possessed the knowledge and power of Omega, there be no concern over exactly how it had come about.

And how could they object, anyway? The cloaking device hadn't just magically fallen into Starfleet's hands. Jim Kirk wasn't above a bit of treachery, not when it was for the greater good.

She heard Bendes's voice out in the corridor. A second later, he walked into the lab with Jim, his first officer, and another dark-haired human in a Starfleet science uniform.

". . . are so few of us, most of the station is closed off," Kettaract was saying. "I think you'll find that everyone here is thoroughly committed to the experiment . . ."

He kept talking, but Jain couldn't hear him. She'd found Jim's gaze and was locked there, searching for some trace of feeling in his watchful eyes. His expression was perfectly neutral, as though he'd never seen her before.

"Ah, Dr. Suni," Kettaract announced, walking the group closer. "I believe you said you've already met Captain Kirk and Mr. Spock. This is Dr. McCoy, the captain's chief medical officer."

The doctor nodded at her, though he, too, seemed preoccupied, his attention moving to the observation booth—where he saw someone he knew, from the look of recognition that crossed his face.

"Captain, that friend I was telling you about . . . would you excuse me a moment?" McCoy asked.

"Go ahead, Bones," Jim said, still watching Jain.

Kettaract was too excited to notice. "Dr. Suni, perhaps you could tell the captain something about what we're doing here, while I show Mr. Spock the equations we're working from . . . ?"

Before waiting for a response, he was already leading Mr. Spock away, describing the equipment, the Vulcan following with his hands clasped behind his back. She and Jim were alone.

"What we're doing is the right thing," she said, not sure what else to say. It was the truth, and the first thing she thought of. "I'm sorry I couldn't tell you before."

"And are you sorry about what happened to Jack Casden?" he asked, studying her, his tone as unreadable as his expression.

So he knew that much. "It was an accident," she said softly, looking away, wishing as she had so many times in the last few days that she'd sent Dickerson instead of Max. Dickerson wouldn't have messed things up. "A mistake."

When she looked at him again, she saw no understanding, no sympathy or even mercy—but there was a hurt deep in his eyes that was painful to look at, and she realized that some part of him had been hoping it wasn't true.

"So this is what you meant, about compromising your beliefs to sustain them," he said, anger tinging his voice. "Killing, so that you and Kettaract could keep working on this, this perfect molecule. Was it worth it? Do you really think that the Federation is just going to wipe out all its enemies when you turn it over to them, that they're going to have the same agenda you do?"

From her guilt and pain, the seeds of frustration took root. She kept her voice low, but the words came sharp and fast. "And you think they won't? Do you really believe that Starfleet will continue to exist by optimism and good intentions alone? Remember what *you* said, about how hard it is to keep the faith when it seems like everyone else is giving up— maybe they're giving up because they finally opened their eyes and realized that a warm smile just isn't going to cut it anymore."

Jim stared at her. "So this is your answer. Lying, stealing, *murdering*."

"Certainly Starfleet isn't capable of anything like that, oh, no," Jain said angrily, struggling to keep her voice down. "Tell me, what's General Order 24? Isn't that the one where you get to destroy an inhabited planet? Starfleet is in denial, Jim, you preach peace and the pursuit of knowledge until anyone comes along who won't follow the rules, and then you break out the phasers and roll right over them."

She stopped to take a deep breath, to regain control. "Don't you see, this *is* the answer. And I'm not the only one who thinks so."

Jim was shaking his head, his gaze hard and unforgiving, but when he spoke he just sounded tired. "All those people, Jain. Casden, his crew—even the man who was investigating. Are you and your friends going to kill everyone who gets too close to finding you out?"

She hadn't heard about Darres, and the news was an unpleasant surprise. It was no wonder Jim wouldn't listen, he had told her that the captain was an old friend.

"I'm sorry about Gage," she said, meaning it. "I didn't know. I swear to you, there's not going to be any more killing, not after today."

Jim looked at her for a long moment, and what she saw in his face was much worse than anger. It was pity.

Without another word, he turned and walked away.

She was standing with a small group near an observation room at the front of the laboratory, older, streaks of gray in her red hair, but otherwise just as he remembered.

McCoy stopped a few meters away, standing uncertainly for a moment as he watched Karen Patterson talking with a short woman, her eyes just as pretty as he remembered. They were actually standing right next to the synthesis space, it seemed, a wide, open area flanked on all sides with heavy equipment. And he realized suddenly that as badly as he'd wanted to find her, to talk to her, now he was afraid.

Because if she tells me there's no cure and no chance of one . . .

McCoy scowled at himself, wondering when, exactly, he'd gone spineless. He straightened his shoulders and went to meet her.

His fear that she wouldn't remember him had been needless. When she saw him approaching, her face lit up.

"Lenny? Lenny McCoy?"

Cringing inwardly—no one had called him Lenny in about a million years, primarily because he despised it—he smiled at her. "Hello, Karen."

She quickly excused herself from her group and took his arm, beaming up at him. "Well, this is a nice surprise. How are you, Lenny? How on earth did you end up out here? Did Bendes talk you into staying for the big event?"

Small talk seemed inappropriate, somehow. He wasn't sure which question to start with, so he decided to ask one of his own. "Karen . . . how did you get mixed up in all this?"

She shook her head, smiling. "I've been wondering that myself. Long story short, a friend of mine, she's a chemist—that woman over there, in the tan blouse? She called me up about six months ago and asked if I was still thinking about pursuing my interest in gamma radiation pathology—which I've been considering for a while now—and she told me about Omega. She sent me the proofs, and I just couldn't resist."

McCoy nodded, but didn't return her smile. "Have you—did you know about the *Sphinx?*"

"What about it?" Her smile slipped. "Nothing has happened to Jack, has it?"

So she didn't know. He shook his head, deciding that there'd be time for that later. "No, I just heard it was the transport out here . . . Karen, aren't you worried about the danger involved in this whole Omega business?"

"No, not really," she said. "I'll admit, I was a little nervous, but only because of just how powerful the molecule will be. Now that the moment is upon us,

I'm actually pretty excited. Everyone is, I've been making the rounds and I'd say the doubt meter is on zero."

She laughed as though she'd told a joke, and McCoy chuckled politely. Same old Karen. He started to tell her that the big moment was probably going to be postponed indefinitely, that the *Enterprise* had come to stop it—but realized suddenly that he just couldn't wait a moment longer, not one. His vaguely prepared story about having a patient with the disease flew right out the window. He had to know, he had to know if there was a chance.

There was no one close by. He faced her, taking a deep breath. "I wanted to find you because I know you spent some time studying xenopolycythemia. I read your paper on it, and you said that there were some promising advances being made . . . I've been diagnosed with it, Karen. Please, tell me honestly— how far away is the cure?"

The unhappy shock on her face gave way to sympathy, compassion . . . but he didn't see what he'd hoped for, what he'd prayed for. There was no reassurance coming.

"Oh, Lenny, I'm so sorry."

McCoy swallowed, hard, and nodded. "That's all right."

"No, I mean I'm sorry you've been diagnosed," she said. "Your chances are slim to none, I won't kid you, but it's not totally hopeless."

Her bedside manner hadn't improved, but he barely noticed. "Really? How, I mean—where? Who's doing the research?"

"You're looking at her," Karen said, though she

wasn't smiling encouragingly. "I've been considering the problem off and on for years, how to slow the red blood cell production. I have a couple of ideas, but Lenny—"

She shook her head. "I don't know. Even if one of them pans out, I just don't know. How long?"

"A year, maybe."

She forced a smile. "Well, I guess I won't be hanging around here, then. I'll pack my bags tonight."

McCoy couldn't believe it. Twenty years had passed, and yet she was willing to set her life aside to help him . . . to offer him a thread of hope, real hope.

The lump in his throat was hard to get past. "I— Karen, I don't know what to say—"

She sighed. "Honestly, Lenny, I wouldn't say anything, yet. I don't want you to get your hopes up."

"Of course," he said, trying to mean it. "I understand."

She opened her mouth to say something else and then stopped, looking past his shoulder. McCoy turned and saw a man approaching, rubbing his nose with one hand and grinning wildly.

"We're ready," he breathed, sniffling loudly, shifting his weight from foot to foot like an overstimulated child. "Everything's ready."

Spock was apparently just finishing looking over Dr. Kettaract's notes when Kirk walked away from Jain to meet them, clamping down on his feelings as best he could.

He was hurt, angry, and dreadfully, horribly disappointed. It was as if she thought he'd never questioned an order, or searched himself for the morality of his choices. She thought he didn't understand, he saw it in her eyes . . . and to be so harshly underestimated by someone he'd respected, shared his feelings with—

She was wrong. He understood exactly what she was saying, what she wanted, what she believed. He'd heard all the arguments before, both sides—the Federation needed to be aggressive and militaristic, it needed to be passive and peaceful. He'd finally come to realize that neither and both were right, and that was the least popular option of all.

He understood that people wanted answers, they wanted solid rules that they could apply to every situation . . . it was the nature of man, he'd always thought, to want to figure everything out in advance. To know how you're supposed to feel and what you're supposed to think without having to constantly question everything, all the time. He wanted it, too, and why not? Everything would be so simple.

And if life actually worked that way, we would all be able to close our minds, to stick to our personal convictions without ever having to listen to anyone else's. To never doubt ourselves . . . but at the expense of never changing.

Starfleet was a military organization. It was also a pacifistic organization, and a scientific one, and many other things . . . and in Starfleet as in life, any situation was best handled by trying to see it with a clear eye before making a choice.

He'd looked at Jain and seen certainty. She'd decided that the Federation needed more power, and had set about trying to achieve it without looking at the decisions she was making to get there. It had been the downfall of too many people to count, and it hurt his heart to see her there.

Kirk stayed standing, though Spock and Kettaract were both seated at a small folding table. Spock set Kettaract's clipboard aside and folded his arms, frowning thoughtfully.

"Well? You see the evolution, don't you?" Kettaract asked eagerly.

"Yes," Spock said. "And the work is brilliant, Doctor. The inclusion of opposing magnetic fields in a cross pattern to more precisely control the acceleration rate is most interesting."

Proud to the point of conceit, Kettaract nodded, smiling. "It is, isn't it?"

"However, your synthesis will almost certainly fail," Spock continued. "The quark-antiquark imbalance will dissolve the atomic binding energy even as it's formed."

Kettaract's smile had faltered. "And I've taken that into account, with the subspace vent at fusion."

"Which will not be sufficient to stabilize," Spock said evenly. "And which will release the reaction into subspace, creating a chain reaction that will have a catastrophic effect on that continuum."

Kettaract shook his head. "That won't happen. The reaction isn't sufficient for the particulate matter to reach a critical velocity, or a critical temperature. The energy will be contained."

Kirk glanced behind him and saw that McCoy had returned, and was watching with some concern.

"According to one of the scientists, everything is ready to go now," Bones whispered, leaning forward. "And they're all convinced it's going to work."

Spock was still speaking. ". . . and while your mathematics are otherwise sound, you've presumed that the transition into subspace will dampen velocity and temperature. I put forth that it will not, and your work hasn't convinced me otherwise."

Jain had approached the other side of the table, to stand behind Kettaract.

"You're arguing a theoretical point," the physicist said angrily.

"Indeed. As are you, Doctor," Spock said. "It is an unknown. You'd be risking your life to find out which of us is right."

"I know—" Kettaract stopped, his face flushed and unhappy . . . and Kirk thought he saw the faintest shadow of doubt cross his face before it was gone.

"The risk is minimal," Jain said, putting her hand on Kettaract's shoulder. "You *know* that. You've worked on Omega for years, you've covered and checked every aspect again and again—we never would have supported you if we didn't believe in your work, Bendes. *I* never would have supported you."

She looked at Kirk, her expression as cold as her voice was encouraging. "Everything is ready to go. Don't let them stop you now, at the very threshold. They don't want anyone to take a chance, because they can't. They're hypocrites, just like the rest of them."

Kettaract was nodding. "You're right, Jain, of course you're right."

"Right or wrong, I'm not going to let you destroy yourselves," Kirk said. If the scientist didn't want to see reason, fine, he didn't have to. "Bones, go talk to your friend, convince her it's over; she can help explain to the others. Spock, start shutting the equipment down, and I'll have Mr. Scott—"

Jain turned and sprinted across the laboratory, running for a long panel set into the wall less than fifteen meters away.

"Captain, she must be stopped!" Spock said, quickly rising to his feet.

Kirk grabbed his phaser, no time to think as he raised it, pointed—

—and Jain was already there, her hand on the panel. He was too late. She turned and smiled triumphantly but there was no happiness in her victory, nothing but self-righteous anger in her expression, crossed with pain when she saw the phaser in his hand.

"I'm sorry, Bendes," she called, her voice ragged. "I know it was supposed to be your big moment."

Kettaract stood up, an incredulous smile breaking across his face. "You did the right thing."

He turned to Spock, still smiling. "We'll find out which of us is right, Mr. Spock, in about ninety seconds."

182

Chapter Sixteen

Jain walked back toward them as a smiling Bendes said something to Spock; she didn't catch it. Probably something about the countdown.

It's done. Finally.

She was still overwhelmed by the sense of relief that had washed over her when she'd flipped the switch; nothing else mattered. Jim Kirk and his high-flying morality could go to hell.

Mr. Spock responded to Kettaract's smiling statement by ignoring it, turning to Jim instead.

"We have to leave immediately, Captain. This station will be destroyed."

"Can we stop it?" Jim asked. "Break the equipment, shut down the computer?"

"Negative, we could accelerate the process."

"I think you should stay for the show," Jain said, but Jim wasn't listening. He snatched up his communicator and flipped it open, talking fast.

"Scotty, lock on to us, prepare to go to warp."

The hum of machinery was filling the room, the other scientists clapping and laughing as they filed into the observation booth.

Jim turned and waved his arms at them, shouting. "Listen to me! You have to evacuate, now!"

"Karen!" the *Enterprise* doctor called, but Dr. Patterson was well inside the booth.

Kettaract started waving, too, shouting louder than either of them. "Everything is fine! Everything is fine! Sixty seconds or less!"

The team members Jain could see looked confused, but they still moved into the booth, finding their seats. She knew they would, they had faith. They knew Kettaract was right. For all his personal failings, he was a genius.

Jim spun around, his frustration absolute, his jaw clenched. "Spock, the ship—"

"We have to leave now, Jim. If we're caught in the initial explosion—"

Jim looked at Jain, his eyes flashing with fear or rage, his expression desperate as he spoke rapidly to his ship. "Five to beam up, and go to warp as soon as you've got us, any direction—"

Kettaract turned and ran toward the booth. Jain backed away, shaking her head. There was no way she was going to miss the miracle, not after all she'd sacrificed, and she'd be damned if she'd let him pull her away. She'd won, they both knew it—but for some reason she just kept seeing the look in his eyes before he'd walked away from her.

How dare *he pity me.*

"We were right to back Kettaract," she said, still backing away. "You'll see."

"Energize," he said, and it wasn't fear or rage in his face as the matter of his form locked, it wasn't pity—but a vast sadness that she couldn't understand, that made her ache just a little, all the same.

He and his men shimmered into glittering energy and were gone.

They'll be back. They'll want to see for themselves.

"Jain! Twenty-five seconds!" Kettaract, at the door to the booth.

She turned and jogged to meet him, arriving just as Dr. Patterson pushed her way back out.

"They're gone?" she asked, definitely upset. "Dr. Angelo said he was calling me—"

Jain shook her head. "They'll be back in a little while," she said. "The captain's science officer gave him some bad advice, that's all."

"Fifteen seconds," Kettaract said, as happy as she'd ever seen him. "Let's take our seats, Doctors."

There were several people talking about the captain's bizarre behavior, a few of them quite concerned, but the anticipation level of the others was higher, and it drowned out the uncertainty. The booth was alive with it, the scientists acting like delighted children.

"Five," Dr. Kettaract said, and the others joined in, counting down. Jain didn't. It was her life she was watching, it was going to be wonderful and powerful and important—and it was all she had.

"Three . . . two . . . one . . ."

It's enough. It's—

Chapter Seventeen

There was no light or sound from the blast of energy, only the light and sound of what it consumed, so quickly that there was no sound at all. The station was enveloped and gone at the speed of light. Everyone and everything on it had disintegrated in less time than it took for the Omega molecule itself to destabilize, .0011 seconds.

There was a blur, a ripple through the dark, an explosion in negative as the antiquarks replicated themselves faster than the quarks, the cloud of nothing expanding, consuming everything it touched.

Chapter Eighteen

"We've got them, sir, but just our people, there wasn't anyone else," Tam said.

The captain had said five, and too bad for the other two, he had his orders. Scott didn't hesitate. "Now, Mr. Sulu."

The *Enterprise* tore away from the station, transitioning smoothly to a steady warp four. Scott was relieved that the captain hadn't specified higher; the power drain from transporting an operational cloaking device had been considerable, though the engineer couldn't imagine that they'd need to move any faster. Explosions could go only so far.

In a matter of seconds, the captain and Mr. Spock were striding onto the bridge. Scotty was happy enough to turn over command, wanting to get to the engineering station and see how his overworked warp reactor was holding up.

"Mr. Sulu," Captain Kirk said, taking his chair. "Prepare a probe."

Scotty quickly checked engineering's emissions numbers, relieved to see that the reaction chamber was just fine. He was about to tell the captain as much when Mr. Spock started talking, bent over to read from his directed monitor.

"The station is gone, Captain," he said, straightening and turning to report, "and there is an expanding relativistic reaction field emanating from where it was. A probe would be ineffective."

"What exactly are we dealing with, Spock?" the captain asked.

"The energy released from the destabilization of this particular molecule is destroying the fabric of subspace," Spock said. "It is creating a dead zone, through which warp travel and subspace communication will be permanently impossible."

"How do we stop it?" the captain asked.

The Vulcan paused, frowning. "Unknown."

He didn't say anything else, and Scotty felt a chill. If Mr. Spock wasn't even prepared to offer a suggestion, it was a difficult situation to be sure.

Captain Kirk turned in his chair to look at him. "What do you mean, unknown? There has to be a way to stop it, to contain it somehow . . ."

"It is currently expanding through subspace at warp two-point-seven and accelerating," Spock said, as calmly as if he were discussing the weather. "The ability to contain such a force is beyond Federation science."

"Then give me *theory,* Spock," Captain Kirk said tersely. "I don't need to know what's not going to work."

"Captain!"

At Sulu's exclamation, they all turned to look at the view screen and for a moment, Scotty couldn't believe what he was seeing, convinced that the sensors feeding the image were malfunctioning. From the coordinates of the Lantaru station, ghost images had formed, like flashes of lightning, a small but steadily expanding patch that radiated and branched outward, fading in and out even as he watched it, the weblike pattern reminding Scott of shattered glass.

He was transfixed. Spock's voice, eerily calm, was the only thing he heard.

"We are witnessing the normal-space 'shadow' of the effect upon subspace," the first officer intoned after checking his station's viewer. "Its speed is now warp three-point-one and accelerating. If it overtakes us while we are in warp, the ship may not survive."

"And if we drop out?" Scott asked.

"Then we will certainly escape destruction, but further use of our warp engines will not be possible while we are inside the dead zone."

Kirk turned to Sulu and said, "Helm, increase speed to warp factor six." The captain continued to watch the screen through narrowed, thoughtful eyes. "Can we stay ahead of it, Spock?"

"Not indefinitely," Spock answered. "I calculate that at the current rate of acceleration, the field will surpass the *Enterprise*'s maximum speed within 41.034 minutes."

"How big will it get?"

"Impossible to say. There is no precedent for Omega destabilization that I'm aware of, and theory alone is unspecific. . . . I project no more than twenty thousand light years before the field dissipates, perhaps less."

Scott cursed beneath his breath, damning Kettaract for causing this, and anyone who'd helped him.

Spock was watching the screen when Kirk suddenly looked at him, rising from his chair and pointing at Spock as he stepped to the railing between them. "You said it was beyond Federation science," the captain said. "What about Romulan?"

Spock arched an eyebrow. "The cloaking device," he said, surmising the captain's meaning.

Kirk nodded. "You've said it works by manipulating gravitons. . . ."

Spock considered it quickly. The cloaking device did indeed use gravitons to bend light. . . . If something was heavy enough it would draw anything, but the specific field of a cloaking device was not designed to create gravity in conventional terms. He and the Romulan commander had discussed the science of it at some length.

But if the device could be modified to attract gravitons through subspace, draw them around the expanding energy field, force implosion using the power from the field—

"Theoretically, it can be done," Spock said. "It will require the addition of a subspace transceiver, and an energy converter that would allow the cloaking device to draw power directly from the field itself. But it would also require the *Enterprise* to position itself dangerously close to the field's wavefront."

"Why?" the captain asked.

"Assuming we can make the necessary modifications for the device to draw subspace gravitons around the field at multiwarp speed, it will have to be very close to the field, and operating when it is beamed into space. Transporting it at all under those conditions will be an incredible strain on the ship's systems, let alone over any distance . . . you must also consider that we'll have to drop out of warp to use a transporter. If it doesn't work, we will either be stranded, or possibly destroyed."

Same prospects as before. Damned if we do, damned if we don't. "I take it you don't have any better ideas?"

An unnecessary question, as Spock certainly would have volunteered a safer and more efficient plan had he thought of one. "No, sir."

"Do it," the captain said, staring out at the Omega effect. "Scotty, help him—and make it fast."

The bridge was silent and grim and Spock and Scotty went below, everyone focused at the screen, watching the irretrievable loss unfold. After the adrenaline-charged emotion of the station—talking to Jain; having had to pull his weapon on her with the intention of shooting; then being hit with the worst helplessness there is, knowing that the people you're looking at will die. After all of that, now they had to wait and watch as a piece of the universe disappeared forever, a nightmare arrangement of the incredible energy source that Jain and Kettaract had dreamed about. More lives lost to their flawed vision. Now the very structure of subspace was being shattered by it.

And if it gets much bigger—

"Mr. Chekov, are there any Federation facilities on this side of the field?" Kirk asked.

The navigator tapped at his console. "Yes, Captain. One mining colony, one science outpost, Tanaris IX and Outpost 771. Both on class-M planets. The field will reach the innermost one, Tanaris IX, in . . . nine minutes."

Damn. He tried to remind himself it could be much worse. It came as no comfort. "Lieutenant Uhura, I want you to send out a broadband message to both facilities, alerting them to the situation. Tell them that if the worst-case scenario occurs, we'll start sending messages immediately at conventional lightspeed . . . but that it may be years before contact can occur."

Uhura nodded, her voice tight with concern. "Yes, Captain."

Kirk resisted an urge to call engineering again, aware that it had been all of three or four minutes since the last time he'd called. Telling Spock and Scotty to hurry one more time might make him feel like he was taking action, but one of them would have to stop what he was doing to report.

All he could do was keep his fingers crossed that they would be able to pull off one more miracle.

Watching the ghost-image of the energy field continue to swell reminded Sulu of a story his grandfather had once told him. Kikani Sulu had been a shuttle pilot on Earth for most of his life, and had collected cultural legends and anecdotes from his stays all over the world.

It was one of those vague childhood recollections that he could only partially recall, sitting across from his grandfather at the dinner table one afternoon, the old man telling the myths he'd heard describing the end of time or the universe, he couldn't remember exactly. What he did remember was something about a goddess giving birth to shadow, the shadow growing up to be darkness. When its mother died, the darkness would strike out in grief and everything would end, forever.

Sulu shuddered and wondered about Dr. Kettaract as he looked again at the spreading dead zone, about the mind that had accidentally given life to such darkness.

Scotty worked as fast as he could, somehow finding a way to link a Federation energy converter and subspace transceiver to the base of the cloaking device. Mr. Spock was manipulating the last of the tiny filaments that were webbed through the globe of the Romulan machine, regularly consulting a propped-up tricorder to montior its patterning sequence.

Scott understood the theory behind Mr. Spock's plan, and knew a lot about coaxing ordinarily incompatible technologies into working together. But he wouldn't have known enough to do this on his own. He'd hardly understood the cloaking device when he'd first hooked it up to the *Enterprise,* and was privately astounded at the time that it had worked at all. But this . . .

They were turning the cloaking device into a lightning rod, one that would attract free gravitons through subspace, essentially compressing them into a forcefield shell against the expanding Omega field. The trapped kinetic energy was supposed to amplify the cloak's effect, creating enough feedback to force a subspace implosion. *If* the device lasted that long.

Scott finished his end only a minute after Mr. Spock resealed the top of the device. Scott flipped a switch, and indicator lights on the transceiver glowed green.

"Scott to bridge. It's finished, captain. Mr. Spock says it should work, but if it doesn't . . ."

"There's no choice, Mr. Scott," the captain said, the stress clear in his voice. "Get it ready to transport immediately, and tell Spock to report to the bridge."

"Aye, sir," Scott said, knowing from the sound of it that it had gotten bad out there while they'd been working. He only hoped that it wasn't about to get much worse; if the graviton lightning rod didn't work, there'd be none of them left to worry about it.

Kirk had Sulu drop out of warp, far enough from the pursuing energy field to allow them a twenty-second countdown. After the seemingly endless and agonizing moments spent watching the swelling destruction, waiting helplessly, Kirk could still only wait and watch. With the lives of his crew now on the line, the seconds felt too short, his thoughts too fast.

"Nineteen . . . eighteen . . ." Spock began, and with the strangely rippling space suddenly tearing toward them, Kirk abruptly remembered his first officer's last countdown only days before—twenty seconds before Sulu had jumped into warp.

To save the Sphinx. The cleanup of a different kind of disaster, less consequential than minimizing the effects of this current force of destruction, maybe, but no less appalling. All those people's lives, and for nothing greater than the barely cloaked cause of aggressive patriotism, fear and greed dressed up as loyalty.

"Thirteen . . ."

The lights of the bridge dimmed significantly as Scotty diverted power from all over the ship to work the transporter, the incredible draw taking its toll. The cloak was already on, but until it began siphoning power from the field, turning the energy against itself, its effectiveness wouldn't be known. If it didn't work, there wouldn't be time to register failure.

"Nine . . ."

The field had grown immense, its curves and far-reaching tangents already engulfing two worlds with hundreds of Federation citizens. They were watching the formation of a scar that would last forever.

Come on—

"Four . . . three . . ."

"Energizing." Scotty.

Two . . . one . . .

"Warp speed, Mr. Sulu!" Kirk ordered.

Sulu's hands moved—

—and suddenly the ship lurched, battered and tossed as the field overtook them. The force knocked Chekov out of his seat, sent Kirk slamming into the railing near Spock's station. On the other side of the bridge, stations sparked and blew out as the hull groaned against the strain. Spock fought to keep his eyes focused on his viewer—

Too late. We were too late—

Then, suddenly, all was calm. The AG and inertial dampeners reasserted stability. Chekov picked himself up, apparently unharmed, and the bridge crew as one began checking the ship's systems. Uhura's voice called for damage and casualty reports throughout the ship.

Spock announced the result calmly. "The energy field has imploded."

Chekov and Sulu both let out held breath, and he could hear some of Scotty's people cheering over the intercom. Uhura reported mostly minor injuries and no fatalities, with minimal damage to the ship. The *Enterprise* had weathered the storm well. Kirk tried to focus on that, and the fact that his crew had survived. They were safe.

And dead in the water.

"The cloaking device did not achieve our purpose as quickly as I'd hoped," Spock offered. "We were overtaken by the field before it could be contained."

Kirk nodded grimly, resigned to years, perhaps decades of sublight travel until they cleared the dead zone. "How long until we can use warp drive again?"

Spock frowned, considering. "Assuming Mr. Scott cannot increase the efficiency of the impulse engines, we will be unable to clear the dead zone for at least nine days."

Kirk felt his eyes widen, fighting and failing to

control the grin spreading across his face. "Nine days," he repeated.

Spock nodded as he looked at Kirk, his eyes *almost* smiling back.

Kirk shook his head and laughed, then turned and settled into his chair, his smile fading as the strain caught up with him, grimly knowing that Bendes Kettaract and Jain Suni would always be remembered for their work, just as they'd wanted.

"Mr. Chekov," he said, "kindly set a course for Deep Space Station M-20. Mr. Sulu . . . best speed."

Chapter Nineteen

Christine knew that something was definitely wrong and four days into the journey out of the Lantaru sector, she was starting to fear that it might be serious.

The doctor hadn't been himself lately, even before he'd lost his friend on that station—that early morning she'd walked in on him, for example, when he'd seemed so evasive. He'd definitely withdrawn further into himself in the days since the Omega affair, though, and while she could understand the pain of losing someone, she thought it went deeper than that. It was as though he was going through the motions of his life, doing the same things he always did but without actually *doing* them. She'd known him too long not to notice his unhappiness, and though she'd always felt that it was rude not to respect other people's privacy, enough was enough.

Since she wasn't a manipulative person by nature,

she gave the approach careful thought, well aware that the doctor rarely gave anything up without a fight. With the crew physicals finally finished and correlated, only the final report left to be turned in, they had a fair amount of unoccupied time; still, she waited until they were both about to go off shift before approaching him. It would keep him from feeling trapped, she hoped, providing him with a fast escape. And when she finally spoke up, she did so with her hands on her hips, ready to drag it out of him with what tools she had.

"Dr. McCoy, you've hurt my feelings," she said sternly, and was glad to see a look of genuine surprise on his face, very different from the slightly dazed look he'd been wearing lately. It was a start.

"I'm—sorry," he fumbled. He obviously had no idea what he was apologizing for, but for as grouchy as he could get sometimes, he was also a gentleman at heart.

"I thought we were friends," she said, hoping she sounded properly wounded.

The doctor blinked. "Ah, I thought so, too."

"And here you've been walking around for days with your chin practically on the ground, and you don't think enough of me to tell me what's wrong," she said.

He finally got it, and the scowl that crossed his face was as real as his surprise had been. She was glad to see that, too.

"Nurse, I don't believe that you're entitled to know about my personal affairs," he said acidly. "That's why they're called ' personal.' "

"You don't trust me," she accused, crossing her

arms tightly. "After all this time, all we've been through together, you still don't trust me."

She had him. He had the same look he'd worn when he'd forgotten her birthday two years before.

"Now, don't be like that."

"Then tell me," she said, finally letting her real concern show through. "Tell me what's wrong, so I can help."

He stared down at the floor. "There's nothing you can do."

"Let me try."

He looked up at her, and after a moment, he nodded. "Let's sit down."

He told her everything. The diagnosis and the prognosis. Remembering his friend Dr. Patterson, and asking Chekov to find her, and then what happened on the station. Christine felt tears welling up early on but managed to hold them back, knowing that if she cried he'd be sorry he told her.

When he was finished, she reached out and took his hand, holding it firmly in hers. "You have to tell the captain," she said. "And not because he needs to know, but because he's your friend."

He shook his head. "I don't know. I thought I might wait . . ."

Christine squeezed his hand. "I *do* know. You need the support of your friends right now, more than anything."

He didn't look convinced but she knew how important it was, knew that she had to push. "Doctor, promise me you'll tell him."

"Of course I'll tell him," he grumbled. "I don't exactly have a choice."

"Soon," she said. "Promise me you'll do it soon. You could tell him when you turn in the physical report."

He sighed, and his sincere sarcasm was back, too. "Fine. Now, if you're finished telling me what to do, would it be all right with you if I left?"

Christine nodded, afraid to speak, knowing her voice would break. He stood up from the chair he'd pushed next to the desk, and watching him put his cantankerous face back on like a mask, she managed a smile for him.

Dr. McCoy didn't say anything, either, but before he left he rested his hand on her shoulder for just a few seconds, and she knew that he was thanking her as well as he could.

She waited until he was gone, buried her face in her hands, and wept.

McCoy went to his quarters. He carefully poked around the edges of how he was feeling for a little while, not quite sure what he was going to find . . . but when he realized he wasn't going to have some sort of melodramatic breakdown, he cut straight to the point.

Karen Patterson was dead, and he was probably going to die soon, and that was a hard truth, but he wasn't going to run from it. He didn't think he was quite ready to embrace it, but maybe that was something a person worked up to, gradually. There were people he didn't want to leave, who he knew would think of him and miss him, and that was more than a lot of people had.

There.

Dr. McCoy suddenly realized that he was hungry, damned near famished, in fact, and decided he'd go get himself something to eat. No point in starving himself to death.

Spock was unable to find his focus.

Usually, he would perceive his lack of concentration as a reason to pursue a deeper meditation, but there were times he recognized as more difficult than others. He opened his eyes and stood, walking to his desk where he sat again, templing his fingers.

It was the thought of his last discussion with the captain that had intruded on his meditation, for what he'd told Spock and what he'd avoided speaking about. Both disturbed him.

First, the captain's report to Starfleet, the report extensive but the gist of it simple. The Omega molecule was too dangerous to be studied. The destructive, long-term consequences for a spacefaring civilization were too great. Two Lantaru-sector colonies had essentially been cut off from the Federation by the damage to subspace, now years away from any kind of contact with anyone, and for that they'd been most fortunate, considering what might have happened. The captain had then recommended that Starfleet Command strongly consider banning any and all future Omega research.

Spock understood the captain's reasoning, and could not disagree with it—as he'd told the Romulan commander himself, the sanctity of life was preeminent in his tenets. But he could not support it, either, and thus an intellectual conflict he'd long struggled with had further defined itself—between his sworn duty, to serve and protect the Federation, and his personal ideology, to faithfully seek knowledge in all its forms. How could he comfortably accommodate both, in consideration of what the Omega molecule had brought to light?

He considered the Romulan commander's understanding of his commitment to duty, reflecting on her perceptions of him when they had been joined. She'd found the disharmony over the theft of the cloaking device, and it had given her relief to know that he struggled still, duty or integrity. Her perception was that without a struggle, without some depth of internal strife, neither held meaning; that to be whole, one had to continually challenge the decisions one made. It was an interesting viewpoint, and he had not yet rejected it.

Ex Astris Scientia. From the stars, knowledge. It was the Starfleet motto, emblazoning the very flag of the Academy, and it had always appealed to him in its simplicity and truth, for the concept it represented. A concept that could very well be betrayed by the Starfleet mechanism—because although he was certain their decision would not be made lightly, Spock thought it highly probable that a prohibition would be issued against Omega research. If they chose to implement the captain's suggestion . . . how could Spock continue to serve without question? If he couldn't have faith that the Federation's most basic article would not be violated, how would his commitments change?

The conflict wasn't new. The Omega impasse simply epitomized it by its extremity, but Spock did not see a logical means to work through it, unless it was by choosing the lesser of two evils. Unfortunately, he didn't know which it was.

What the captain had not discussed—logical conclusions from evidence that had presented itself throughout the *Sphinx*/Kettaract situation—indicated only that he was not yet prepared to broach the subject. It was quite clear that Jim was wrestling with a loss of certitude in the things he held dear, and although there was the possibility for most in those circumstances, that evidence would be ignored in favor of tranquility, Spock knew that he would not falter. The captain's consistency of character required that he would always choose truth over peace of mind.

Spock himself recognized that everything changed, and that some incidental results were inevitable.

Chapter Twenty

The captain sat in his chair gazing at the main screen, his thoughts far away.

He thought about all that had happened in recent days, about the decisions that were sometimes made, when someone couldn't accept that what they had was enough. He thought about the implications of a few things Jain had said, and about the message his old friend had tried to get to him. He could feel himself fighting against the conclusion that he was slowly coming to, that perhaps the two were connected, fighting it as much by reflex as by choice. He knew he would lose.

He watched the freezing dark slip by, knowing that things were different for him now, that there'd been a fundamental shift in how he perceived things, and that he could never go back. He was deeply immersed in an unsettling scrutiny of himself and what he was trying to protect, so much so that he didn't notice either his first officer or the ship's doctor when they stopped by to see him, both of them troubled with reflections all their own. Each man lingered next to him for a moment or two before slipping away, leaving him be.

The soft, lulling sounds of the bridge soothed his tired mind a little, but not quite enough to let him rest easy.

Epilogue

TWO MONTHS LATER

When Kirk finally arrived at the tavern, they were all there, waiting. Five men in civilian clothes, inhabitant's clothes, just like his, sitting at a scuffed wooden table in the back room. The tavern he'd chosen was nowhere special, a town that no one had ever heard of on a planet no one ever visited. It was exactly the right place to have a meeting that didn't exist, a meeting that had taken weeks to bring about.

Kirk sat down, smiling, glad to see them all regardless of the circumstances. "Gentlemen. Have introductions been made?"

Phil Waterston, captain of the *U.S.S. Constitution*, shook his head. "I don't know about everyone else, but I just got here."

Kirk introduced them to one another, even knowing that a few had met before. Commodore Bob

Wesley. Commodore Aaron Stone. Captain Nick Silver. Commodore Jose Mendez. Captain Waterston. There were nods of recognition, smiles, a handshake where it was convenient.

A young boy, a native of the planet, wandered back to ask what they wanted. At the shrugs from the others, Kirk asked for a pitcher of the local brew, a kind of fermented grain drink from what he could gather.

As soon as the boy was gone, Silver spoke up. "Talk to us, Jim. What's this about?"

Kirk reached into the lining of his shirt and pulled out a hardcopy of the Starfleet Charter. A part of it, anyway, sections 28 through 34 printed out on a single sheet of paper. He handed it to Wesley, sitting to his left.

"I'd like each of you to read section 31, carefully," he said. "It's short, it won't take long."

Their server brought back a brimming pitcher and a half-dozen mugs before disappearing again. Kirk filled the mugs as the hardcopy was passed around the table, Stone reading last. When he raised his head, looking as confused as the rest of them, Kirk began his story.

It took a few minutes and he didn't like telling it, but he left nothing out, starting with the line from section 31 that rather obscurely referred to the establishment of "an autonomous investigative agency," one that held nonspecific discretionary power over nonspecific Starfleet matters. Hidden in plain sight.

From there, Jack Casden and the *Sphinx*. The possibility that Admiral Cartwright and perhaps Commodore Jefferson had been involved in a plot to get the cloaking device and then keep its use a secret, knowingly or unknowingly. Kettaract's politics, and the death of Gage Darres. The Lantaru station, and the terrible accident that had occurred there, that was responsible for the Omega Directive, only just instituted for Starfleet flag officers. He told them about everything . . . except for Jain, of course, because that part of it still hurt, and because it wasn't necessary for them to know about her. And he avoided bringing up Bones's near brush with death. The disease the doctor had diagnosed during the crisis had since been cured, thanks to their discovery of the Fabrini medical archive.

When he'd finished, no one spoke for a moment. He could see some skepticism, some doubt—but he also saw five good men, men he would trust with his life . . . and he believed that each of them might say the same about him.

Mendez cleared his throat, looking unhappily at Kirk. "You realize what you're telling us, what you're saying."

"I do."

Wesley shook his head in disbelief . . . but Kirk could see beneath it, could see that he just didn't *want* to believe. Kirk knew exactly how he felt.

"You're telling us that there's a shadow agency operating *within our ranks,* Jim, and has been for over a century—how sure are you about this?"

Kirk raised his hands, motioning at their group. Three commodores, three captains, each of them with established lives in different sectors, commands in different parts of the galaxy. "You tell me."

He watched it sink in, watched each of them

struggle against the idea just as he had struggled. A part of him, an innocence, had died when he'd accepted the truth, and he hated that he was asking them to do the same, to sacrifice their trust in the sanctity of their home—because that's what Starfleet was, to all of them.

"So what are you proposing?" Waterston asked. "It sounds like we won't even be able to prove that this 'Section 31' exists."

Stone was nodding. "If all this is true, they've already done a good job covering their tracks. There's not even any evidence, is there?"

Kirk shook his head. "No. And I doubt that there's going to be any, not now. Maybe not for a long time. They're careful, whoever they are, very careful, and it appears that they have the resources to keep doing what they're doing. Which is why I propose no action at all—"

He quickly pressed on before anyone of them could respond, well aware of what each man was thinking. Hadn't he thought the same things?

"—because it won't work, we don't have anything on them, and if this is the type of group I think it is, bringing this out in the open means they disappear," Kirk said, looking seriously at each man in turn, knowing their frustration as his own. "Gone, faster than we can point a finger. For now, all we can do is wait for them to make a mistake. And they will . . . maybe not this year, or next, but nobody can hide forever."

"Why this meeting, then?" Mendez asked. "If there's nothing we can do . . ."

"Because there is something you can do," Kirk

answered. "Something that I should have done, when I first got the order from Admiral Cartwright, when I knew—I *knew*—that something wasn't right. What you can do is keep your eyes open. What you can do is listen, and watch, and tell the people you trust to do the same.

"I'm convinced that what Starfleet stands for is good and true, and I think this Section 31, whatever it is, exactly, is only a very small part—like a tumor, a cancer. Something that doesn't reflect any of the virtues and beliefs that Starfleet is about. But if each of you—each of us—is willing to question that one order that doesn't feel right, if we are willing to accept the responsibility of keeping our faith, by no longer taking it for granted—if we're willing to do that, then the cancer won't be able to spread."

He spoke the rest only in his mind. *All it requires is accepting that there's something hiding in the shadows, in the darkness that you didn't even know existed. Oh, and losing some of your innocence—but it doesn't hurt for very long.*

The six men talked for a while longer, but everything had been said that needed to be. One by one, they left the tavern to return to their lives, perhaps not as shining and pure as they had thought them before, until only Kirk remained.

He sat, thinking, for long time. Finally, as the shadows began to stretch across the floor, the captain picked up his mug and toasted the empty air, setting it down again without drinking. He dropped a few coins on the table and walked out, wondering if any of it was worth anything at all, knowing at his core that it was.

About the Author

S. D. (Stephani Danelle) Perry writes multimedia novelizations in the fantasy/science-fiction/horror realm for love and money. She is the author of *Avatar,* the two-volume relaunch of the *Star Trek: Deep Space Nine*® novels, which begins the arc of stories set after the TV series. She's also a two-time contributor to the acclaimed short-story anthology *Star Trek: The Lives of Dax.* Her other works include the best-selling *Resident Evil* series of novels, several *Aliens* novels, as well as the novelizations of *Timecop* and *Virus.* Under the name Stella Howard, she's written an original novel based upon the television series *Xena, Warrior Princess.* She lives in Portland, Oregon, with her husband and beloved dogs.

Look for STAR TREK fiction from Pocket Books

Star Trek®: The Original Series

Star Trek: Deep Space Nine®

Star Trek®: New Frontier

Star Trek®: Invasion!

#1 • *First Strike* • Diane Carey
#2 • *The Soldiers of Fear* • Dean Wesley Smith & Kristine Kathryn Rusch
#3 • *Time's Enemy* • L.A. Graf
#4 • *The Final Fury* • Dafydd ab Hugh
Invasion! Omnibus • various

Star Trek®: Day of Honor

#1 • *Ancient Blood* • Diane Carey
#2 • *Armageddon Sky* • L.A. Graf
#3 • *Her Klingon Soul* • Michael Jan Friedman
#4 • *Treaty's Law* • Dean Wesley Smith & Kristine Kathryn Rusch
The Television Episode • Michael Jan Friedman
Day of Honor Omnibus • various

Star Trek®: The Captain's Table

#1 • *War Dragons* • L.A. Graf
#2 • *Dujonian's Hoard* • Michael Jan Friedman
#3 • *The Mist* • Dean Wesley Smith & Kristine Kathryn Rusch
#4 • *Fire Ship* • Diane Carey
#5 • *Once Burned* • Peter David
#6 • *Where Sea Meets Sky* • Jerry Oltion
The Captain's Table Omnibus • various

Star Trek®: The Dominion War

#1 • *Behind Enemy Lines* • John Vornholt
#2 • *Call to Arms...* • Diane Carey
#3 • *Tunnel Through the Stars* • John Vornholt
#4 • *...Sacrifice of Angels* • Diane Carey

Star Trek®: The Badlands

#1 • Susan Wright
#2 • Susan Wright

Star Trek®: Dark Passions

#1 • Susan Wright
#2 • Susan Wright

Star Trek®: Section 31

Cloak • S. D. Perry
Rogue • Andy Mangels & Michael A. Martin
Abyss • Dean Weddle & Jeffrey Lang
Shadow • Dean Wesley Smith & Kristine Kathryn Rusch

Star Trek® Books available in Trade Paperback

Omnibus Editions

Other Books

STAR TREK®

STICKER BOOK

MICHAEL OKUDA
DENISE OKUDA
DOUG DREXLER

POCKET BOOKS
A VIACOM COMPANY

STAR TREK

isbn: 0-671-01472-2   STKR